THE MOSAIC MAKER AND THE BOAT BUILDER

THE MOSAIC MAKER AND THE BOAT BUILDER

BARBARA KINGHORN

Barbara Kinghorn Kerygma Publishing

Contents

Dedication

To Rocky and Denise Wallace -
good representatives of committed family members and
church workers who have sown in tears.

We knew the name Kirklin Durand was significant,
so we drove near the border and found Kirklinton.

When God gives a name, it lasts forever.

Their souls will always be part of us within the Body of Christ
that transcends earth and heaven.

Kirklin Durand - Enduring, Lasting Church

Special thank you to Joseph and Anna Keren Kinghorn
for making the book cover design possible.

I

A Veil O'er the Past

Why are you cast down, O my soul?
And why are you disquieted within me? -Psalms 42:11a NKJV

Urtzi emerged from a side porch of the urban dwelling where friends had gathered to celebrate his wedding. His eyes saw nothing in the courtyard but his bride, Esuvia, who had just arrived from the procession that had begun that morning at her childhood home. Her thick auburn tresses were folded and plaited behind the yellow veil, with only gorgeously twirled tendrils peeping out to grace the sides of her fair face. He moved toward her and took her hands in his. Joyful whispers were heard round the group of admiring guests. It struck him that the whispers had almost an ethereal quality, as if angels and Heaven's occupants were present to commend the ceremony.

At that moment, Esuvia's aunt theatrically pulled a white linen tablecloth from a basket and with her daughter's assistance raised it in the breeze. With elaborate timing and gracious gestures, they lowered the cloth over a wooden table by the portal of Urtzi's house. Her father then placed an elaborately decorated pot of animal grease on the center of the table. The object was covered in a mosaic design by the bride herself, and it would be used to complete the ceremony as Esuvia walked through the doorway of Urtzi's home to begin their new life together.

Esuvia lifted her gentle brown eyes to Urtzi's gaze with such trusting earnestness, only to note that his countenance had suddenly saddened. His lips trembled and tears of pain welled up that he squeezed away with a squint and a brush of his hand. Her visage mirrored the expression of grief that came over him, but the couple hid their emotions from those nearby, gazing into each other's faces with troubled seriousness that was mistaken for sincerity by onlookers. No one seemed to notice the loss of joyful radiance that should have glowed between them in that moment.

After a nod from Urtzi, Esuvia proceeded to the doorpost of the house where she dipped her hand into the pot of animal grease without reservation and generously smeared it on the portal sides. Smiling again briefly, she glanced round at the guests who cheered and lifted goblets of wine to encourage her.

Urtzi then approached her and handed her a goblet. She raised it to the guests, and they cheered even more enthusiastically. He then took her hand and gently escorted her into the passage.

"Enjoy the wedding feast!" he said broadly to the crowd and without meeting their eyes, Urtzi closed the heavy wooden door. The courtyard then rocked with shouts of laughter.

But Urtzi turned to Esuvia with distress etched across his face. The smile she had temporarily recovered vanished again, and she suddenly grasped his face with her hands.

"Urtzi, what is the matter?" she half cried in a loud whisper.

His face mirrored an internal struggle, and he covered his mouth with his hand. Then he took Esuvia's arm and steered her away from the door into another room. There, he sat down on a bench and began to sob quietly.

Esuvia was astounded. Of all the scenes she had imagined on her wedding day, this was not one she had ever envisioned. For several moments, she stood speechless. Then she sat down beside him on the bench and instinctively placed her arm around his shoulder while gently clasping his other shoulder with her hand. She placed her face close to his and said, "Urtzi, what can I do to help you? Are you displeased with me?"

Urtzi gave one shake of his head and muttered, "No, Esuvia, I am not displeased with you."

"Was there a guest in the crowd who upset you?" she persisted.

Again, he shook his head. "No, I am not upset with any guest."

"Are you afraid of anything? Are you feeling unwell?" she queried.

"No, darling. I simply ... saw an object that triggered a ... a terrible memory." He paused, and suddenly fled to a plant pot where he retched over and over.

Esuvia was stunned. Urtzi had never mentioned any past trauma during the years of sharing meals, discussing their work, and growing up together as neighbours. Finally, she asked another question while maintaining a calm exterior, but inwardly feeling sickened by fear of something dreadful that Urtzi had hidden from her. "Can you tell me what the memory is about?"

Urtzi shook his head. "It is a memory of something I observed from a distance a very long time ago, long before we met. I witnessed a scene of a horrible misfortune that was not unlike misfortune that befell my own family in childhood. I do not want to trouble others with these horrors. These memories are all ... a jumbled mass that weighs heavily on my mind. One scene flows into another scene, and there are triggers that make my emotions overwhelm me. Many things happened before I met you. Be assured that my distress has nothing to do with you."

Esuvia was shocked and withdrew her embrace for a moment. The word "horrors" had lodged in her mind and made her throat tighten with dread. She continued to pry for answers. "Urtzi ... we are married now. You must be honest with me. What on earth could a man remember in such a way that the scene within your mind would ruin your wedding ceremony?"

Urtzi shook his head again, but he could not dislodge the thoughts within his head. "I apologize, Esuvia. I realize that I can never recreate that once-in-a-lifetime moment of our wedding ceremony. I am so sorry for having spoiled it for you." He quietly wept some more from remorse.

Esuvia had loved Urtzi for a very long time, and so she compassionately insisted that he had not ruined their wedding ceremony. But then, he strangely withdrew alone to another room of the house. He turned to her before closing the door and stated, "I do not want to keep retching before you. I feel physically ill. But be assured, dear Esuvia, all that I have is now yours, my bride. We are greatly blessed, yet I feel very tired just at this moment and must rest to overcome this. Perhaps rejoin the guests and enjoy some of the meal. I will join you later today. We have our entire lifetime to celebrate our union. I am sorry that I must pause for my breath for a short time."

The sound of the wood shutting against the stone echoed through the hall. Esuvia stood staring at the inanimate barricade that firmly separated her from her newly wed husband. Then she wilted into a small heap on the floor and wept with profound disappointment, trying to push feelings of betrayal from her head.

When half an hour had passed and Urtzi had not emerged to comfort her, Esuvia also withdrew into a different room. And both bride and bridegroom lay in separate rooms on their wedding day, under a heavy cloud of sadness.

***

The day that Urtzi had first stumbled upon the lovely Esuvia was a better moment in time. It seemed almost magical in both of their memories. Esuvia had gone with her father Tessera to the beach to comb the sand for shells for the mosaics they created for their family trade. Esuvia was kneeling near the sloppy surf designing a template as her father walked up and down the shore gathering materials. The ocean waves swirled in and out, evoking peaceful admiration with their shapes, and sounds, and offerings left upon the shore. Strands of ginger hair hung over Esuvia's eyes as she focused her entire energy upon the art before her.

With the careless sea breeze in his head, Urtzi had ambled over to Esuvia's circle of items she was shaping into the vision in her mind's eye. After several minutes, she became aware of the shadow near her and, cupping her hand over her brow, she squinted into the bright sunlight that hid Urtzi among purple and white flashes playing with her eyes. Neither of them spoke until he impishly nudged a seashell with his toe, upsetting the balance of her picture. Without thinking, she sniffed with fake disdain, picked up a handful of wet sand, and flung it at his knees. He feigned offense and wordlessly walked away. For a long time, Esuvia stared after him until he became a tiny shape far in the shimmering distance.

It was not long before it was established that Urtzi was working in the seaside town assisting with boatbuilding teams. Esuvia passed him rather often and noted that her father learned of the recently arrived young labourer and spoke of him with respectful regard for his skill and work ethics.

Urtzi never missed an opportunity when Esuvia walked by him to jest a bit. In turn, she pretended to create a wide berth between them, but never missed the moment to glance back over her shoulder with an expressionless face while he smirked and twinkled his eyes at her. Then she would flounce her hair behind her and swagger away in the opposite direction of him with an air of determination to avoid his attention.

"So, what is the name of the boy who walked out of the sea?" she asked her father, Tessera, one day as she lay the table for supper.

Tessera worked alongside her distributing fish he had just cooked over an open fire outside. "The boy who walked out of the water is named Urtzi. He appears to be Vasco (Basque), but he travelled to our town by river, not by sea. He may be of foreign descent, but he has been living in this region his entire life. He was the second generation born here after his grandparents immigrated here from Vasco. His grandfather was a Roman soldier who helped to build *Valium Aelium* (Hadrian's Wall)."

"How would you know that?" Esuvia furrowed her brow.

Tessera stoked the kitchen hearth fire and stirred a pot of stewing vegetables. "I asked him."

"Why do you believe him?"

"Why would I not believe him? He is a clean-living and earnest young man. Everyone can see that in his face and responsible actions."

Esuvia nodded and muttered, "Mm."

"He seems to be alone, so we should perhaps invite him for a meal sometime," Tessera continued.

"Where does he live?" Esuvia inquired.

"Maybe nowhere in particular. He may live in the tents by the river where others like him dwell. He has no family and no connections, but he possesses the ability and willingness to work with his hands. He probably spends his earnings to buy food."

And indeed, this was Urtzi's challenging plight for a while. The meals that Esuvia and Tessera shared with him often were welcome, as was the friendship for which he hungered. But he grew in stature in every way with the passing seasons.

One day, Esuvia missed him as she walked her usual route on errands. Urtzi had quietly saved his boatbuilding wages and acquired a room of a house. The house belonged to another boatbuilder, one not unlike himself. The house owner, Adrian, was an elder and in need of some assistance, and Urtzi could be trusted with that task.

For two more years, Urtzi worked for him, and then Adrian died, having willed his house to Urtzi, since neither of them had any surviving relatives after the plague. The orphaned grandson of immigrants who began his adult life by building boats and living in a refugee camp in ancient Britannia grew to become a property owner and a trusted townsman. And Tessera and Esuvia had walked beside him with sincere respect every step of his journey.

***

Sometimes in the evening when the sun lay on the horizon where the sea faded jades, blues, and periwinkle shades into the sky, Urtzi would appear at the door of the workshop where Esuvia and her father prepared supplies for mosaics and designed templates. He would tease and harass Esuvia, asking why she placed that material there when it obviously belonged somewhere else. She would roll her eyes at him and chase him away with equal amounts of pretended abuse about his boat designs.

Then, as dusk set in upon one of those glowing endings of a day and peach-coloured wisps of cloud rolled across the sky, Urtzi tiptoed into the workshop behind Esuvia and cast a small plate before her. On the plate he had amateurly designed a mosaic of the head of a girl with ginger tresses. Large brown eyes shone warmly from her face and a smile hinted from the corners of her mouth. She wore a necklace with a locket representing her maiden status.

Esuvia sat silently staring at the childish and yet poignant art. Suddenly she felt tears filling her eyes, and she blinked them away before she glanced up at Urtzi to see if he had an explanation to offer. He was watching Esuvia in return to see how she would react. For a moment, they both looked at one another without any words.

Finally, Esuvia cleared her throat and asked plainly, "This is me? Why did you depict me? That must have taken you a long time."

"It only filled the hours I always spend thinking of you," Urtzi replied quietly. His heart was pounding so hard, he was breathless.

Esuvia cast her eyes back at the mosaic feeling uncertain of how she should reply. She could not explain what moved her about the unexpected gesture, but the feeling was not unwelcome.

"Do you ever think of me, Esuvia? If you do not, could you begin to think of me as more than a neighbour who drops in for dinner and ungratefully criticizes your art?"

Esuvia felt gladness in her heart, and she eventually nodded. "Yes, that would be a welcome change, especially if you stop criticizing my art!" she added with a laugh.

Urtzi's face broke into an all-encompassing beam of joy. And from that moment, their childhood banter that had always bordered on annoyance and rivalry transformed into a more mature and mutually supportive love commitment. But the jesting in their chemistry would never end.

"One day, I shall turn up at your boatyard with a carving of wood. Of course, it won't be very well-carved since I am neither a carver nor a boatbuilder. Nevertheless, I will impose this gift upon you. It will be a boat with the figurehead of a merman at the helm. And he will have the face of a Vasco!" she quipped when Urtzi was ready to depart for his house after dinner.

"Handsome indeed!" Urtzi remarked.

She glanced over her shoulder at him with an expressionless face, then tossed her head in the usual way and set about washing some dishes. She did not hear Urtzi steal up behind her and was startled when she turned around and saw he was only an inch from her face. He quickly kissed her cheek and disappeared out the door into the night. Tessera joined in the laughter, also filled with the joy of the love between his daughter and the very good neighbour who had walked out of the water and was fast becoming like a son to him.

***

Now, she was his bride, and Esuvia was pounding again on the heavy door. "Urtzi! It has been three days!"

She had faced the guests at the feast alone with a strained smile and uncertain look in her eyes. Thanking each for coming and fielding off their surprise at her appearance alone without Urtzi by her side, she explained he would come later after a little rest. He never did though, and each guest left one by one, having enjoyed the fare but feeling something was perhaps amiss.

One night, two nights, three nights passed, and Esuvia was beginning to despair. Her relatives had also gone home, and she was left to absorb the cold silence of the nearly empty house. Urtzi's reassurances were very minimal. He would only reply to her calls to him through the door with quiet utterances of, "I will be up later. If you need anything, go to market and buy what you must."

At first, she had gone into the room and lain down beside him. He faced the wall and remained immoveable. Then he would shake with sobs and ask her to leave.

Four nights, five nights, and Esuvia's heart had become gripped within a metal vise so strong, she thought she would die. Her throat was squeezed nearly shut so that she could barely swallow. Her eyes were constantly hot with fearful tears. He had heard her sobbing and wailing for days, and now she began to shout.

"It has been a week, Urtzi! If you do not emerge from the room today, I am going back home to my father!"

This was met with silence.

"What will you do? I have no understanding of what the matter is! The lively young man I agreed to marry seems to have been an illusion! How long have you been doing this? I thought you worked! Goodbye, Urtzi! I am leaving today!"

More silence.

"And yet, I fear for you, Urtzi! You will eventually die if you refuse to eat or move again! Should I truly leave? You tell me!"

Nothing.

Esuvia began to pound and kick the door, and then to throw objects at it. She hurled a plate and it shattered upon the stone floor. "Don't worry, Urtzi! I am just breaking plates for my mosaic art! I will use the broken pieces rather than seashells!" she taunted as she threw plate after plate at the frame. Then she broke into screaming sobs, rhythmically chanting, "Come out at once! Come out at once! Come out at once!"

Eventually her throat bled from the strain of shouting, and she found she could not clear it easily. She leaned against a far wall, and tears streamed down her face. Just then, the door creaked and moved two inches.

Urtzi's eyes peered through the small crack. "Esuvia ... I need a healer. Do you know anyone? Do you know a doctor? I am so sorry. You are right. I can barely move and have no desire to eat. My head is filled with a thick, grey heaviness. I have never been so miserable. It is not you, though. You must understand that you have not caused this."

For a moment, Esuvia wanted to charge at the door shrieking, "Don't you dare partronize me! Oh, I KNOW I have not caused this! No, YOU have caused this, Urtzi! I do not blame myself!"

But she stopped herself out of the true love she felt for her husband. What if he truly were so sick that he would die without proper care? She took five deep breaths before she spoke with a measure of gentleness.

"Perhaps I should go get father. Or we can go to him together. He can tell us what to do."

"Esuvia ... I don't know if I can walk that far."

They stared at one another wordlessly for several more moments. Finally, Esuvia had an idea. "I will pay a messenger to go and ask him to come."

***

It took several hours for the messenger to travel to Tessera's house, for Tessera to stop his work, and then return to Urtzi and Esuvia's home. He also took the time to go fetch his sister, Priscilla - the aunt who had been a mother figure to Esuvia whose own mother had died in childbirth. Darkness was bringing its heavy weight upon the already shadowed home when Tessera and Priscilla arrived.

Priscilla whisked in, lowering her head cloth to the position of a scarf around her neck with one gesture communicating her readiness to work on the young couple's behalf. Merely the mention of dredging up the memories again in a description to those coming to his mental health aid had caused Urtzi to begin retching again. Tessera and Priscilla walked in to a scene of Esuvia urging Urtzi to swallow some broth she was attempting to spoon-feed him.

The forlorn expression on the face of his daughter who should have been radiant with new love sparked both confusion and anger in Tessera. He stood by the door as if a quick exit might be necessary for him.

Priscilla was more emboldened to speak into the situation. She took a place beside her niece on the edge of the bed where Esuvia sat urging

Urtzi to eat. She placed her hands on Esuvia's sagging shoulders and looked compassionately into Urtzi's face.

"Son, we know something is troubling you deeply, and we know the trouble has not been caused by Esuvia. Yet, she is truly suffering with you, and so we must see what can be done to help you regain your strength of body and mind."

She produced a loaf of bread from beneath her shawl. Urtzi's eyes widened and he began to panic, weeping with uncontrollable, gasping grief. "The bread ... the bread ... the tablecloth ... " barely inaudible words formed.

The family was stunned. After a moment, Priscilla folded the bread under her shawl again. "I can remove the bread, but I see no tablecloth in this room."

Urtzi clutched his sides and continued to shake.

Esuvia, finally supported by the presence of others, tried to stroke Urtzi's hair. "Urtzi, do you mean the tablecloth at the wedding?"

"Yes, it was the linen in the ceremony that caused such vivid pictures!" he stammered.

Priscilla nodded slowly, recalling the look on Urtzi's face, as if a veil came down when she lowered the cloth onto the table for the ceremonial pot of grease display.

"Can you tell us what you are seeing in the pictures, dear son?" she asked softly.

"No ... no I cannot!" Urtzi cried.

"Dear son, we want to help you. Please help us understand," she continued gently.

"No ... I do not understand. I cannot make you understand what I cannot explain."

"Did someone hurt you with a linen cloth?" Esuvia tried.

"No, I have never even touched a linen cloth in my lifetime as a poor child," Urtzi insisted.

"Did a maker of cloth cause you harm?" Esuvia tried again.

"No ... but ... a maker of cloth was harmed ... so greatly harmed!" He winced in emotional agony.

Priscilla and Esuvia exchanged glances.

"Can you tell us, dear son, how the clothmaker was harmed?"

Suddenly Urtzi roared, and everyone in the room began to cry. It was too dark, too much for them all. They knew they could ask no further questions. They sat in silence, overwhelmed by helplessness.

"We must send for a healer," Tessera finally spoke. "Daughter, your aunt will tend to your own needs. You also must eat and rest. I will sleep here on a cot in this room and not leave Urtzi alone in such distress."

Urtzi continued to lie on his side quietly sobbing. Priscilla coaxed Esuvia up and guided her gently from Urtzi's side to a quiet room. Priscilla also would watch over her charge, preparing food for her and resting nearby to provide a reassuring presence. They would send for a healer on the morrow.

2

Throwing Treasure at Dark Water

Who shut up the sea behind doors when it burst forth from the womb, when I made the clouds its garment and wrapped it in thick darkness, when I fixed limits for it and set its doors and bars in place, when I said, 'This far you may come and no farther; here is where your proud waves halt'?
- Job 38:8-11 NIV

Angi, a local healer nicknamed after the Roman healing and snake goddess Angitia, greatly enjoyed the awe of the townspeople for her healing arts. She was an herbalist who relied almost entirely on her keen observational and intuitive skill and was loved for her insightful capacities that often yielded positive outcomes. She visited Urtzi and Esuvia's house, watched the dynamic between the couple and family members assembled to help, and listened to the strange story. Her eyes glittered with comprehension when Esuvia's reaction to the long days and nights of silence was relayed.

At first, Angi prescribed nothing more than calming drinks for both Urtzi and Esuvia. She made them sit together, intertwine their arms, and offer the drinks from cups simultaneously to one another. Among the herbs she used in her potions were bay leaf, sage, chamomile, and lavender. These did work to ease some of their anxiety, and when she had gained their trust to provide some remedies, she advanced to a more complex cure.

"Urtzi, you and your new bride Esuvia are both grieving. You are grieving over a tragedy you once witnessed because you buried the memory before you healed from the experience. Esuvia is grieving not only for you, but also because her dreams began to die only minutes after your wedding ceremony, and even during the ceremony when she first noticed the onset of your deep distress. Though you were not expecting the assault on your mental health, and though you mean no harm whatsoever to Esuvia, your recovery must begin now, or more parts of her will die.

She has been chosen by something beyond herself to shepherd you on a journey of healing. She is an artist. Anger is a part of grief. Her anger at grief for robbing you both was expressed in her plate throwing as she shouted to you through the heavy barrier between you represented by the door. She shouted that the broken pieces would become a new mosaic. The plates hammering at the door did rouse you from your descent into darkness and caused the barrier to crack open so light could begin to enter. Now she, the mosaic maker, will go with you on your journey to find the missing pieces of the broken picture in your mind.

You are a boatbuilder. You were married to a journey long before you married your bride. Journey is part of your soul.

Some healing is counterintuitive. One must sometimes do the opposite of that which feels safe to be healed. Because you are not moving, you must embrace extreme action. Urtzi, you must go on a pilgrimage."

"A pilgrimage?"

"Yes, you must pilgrimage to the place where the tragedy occurred. The veil to the past you were covering came down with the settling of the white linen tablecloth at your wedding ceremony. Therefore, you must take your new bride and pilgrimage to that place of the vivid images in your mind, and face it with courage."

Priscilla, Tessera, Esuvia, and Urtzi all heard the prescription. The room was filled with nervous glances, sharp intakes of breath, whispers, and yet, a settling understanding that Angi's answer was actually correct. Esuvia quickly moved to grasp Urtzi's limp hand, and appealing deeply with her eyes she said, "Urtzi, we must."

Urtzi looked blank for several moments. His demeanor was very listless since he had taken little food for a week. But overwhelmed with the need to find answers or waste completely away, and encouraged by the care of those gathered around him, he slowly nodded. For the first time since the wedding day, he connected to Esuvia with his eyes meeting hers.

A feeling of relief went round the room. Everyone was nodding and half-smiling. Then Angi produced several broken pieces of the plates Esuvia had thrown at the door. "Esuvia, you and your husband must take these broken pieces and begin to create a mosaic as part of your healing. Let us proceed to the porch. I have prepared a space for you to begin a design together."

So all walked gently into the garden air, supporting Urtzi who bravely rose and accompanied his bride forward. More broken plates were laid about a square drawn with chalk. The couple knelt over the art supplies and whispered their ideas. They agreed upon a sunrise to represent a new beginning and set about breaking more pieces with a hammer and arranging them into a completely new image. After a few minutes, a rough template of a design had formed, and the tiny crowd clapped and reached out to touch the couple's shoulders with encouragement. The couple looked warmly into one another's eyes and exchanged light kisses.

Then Angi was compensated with both financial payment and praise for her medical wisdom. "Now, you must eat!" Angi admonished Urtzi. "Your generous offering to me calls for celebration. I shall take a portion of this payment, buy food, and prepare a meal for you so that your strength may begin to be restored. And Esuvia, you must assist me with this healing dinner."

"How can we thank you? Your continued service is beyond what is required," Tessera waved his arm broadly to demonstrate the mutual generosity being shared between Angi and the entire family.

Angi clicked her tongue to silence the protests, pulled a scarf round her head, grabbed Esuvia's arm, and swept out the door with the patient's bride for the market. For the first time since the morning of her wedding day, Esuvia actually laughed.

While they scoured the town for restoring ingredients such as cabbage, barley, plantain, and meat for a sacrifice, Tessera walked Urtzi around the courtyard, and Priscilla stoked a fire in the kitchen. By the time Angi and Esuvia returned, a kettle of water was boiling, and Urtzi was washed and changed. The fresh beginning was tangible.

The family knew nothing of Christus. They offered their meat that evening as a sacrifice to Roman gods before consuming it. Then they drank deeply of wine and sang a hymn to Circe, the snake goddess Angitia's sister. Moved by the family's gratitude, Angi suggested they also thank Celtic deities. Esuvia symbolically offered her girlhood locket to be thrown in a body of water as a thanksgiving that she was passing from one part of life to another.

"Yes, let us process to the water's edge!" Angi cried. "This second celebratory procession will bring restoration to the joy that failed after the wedding day procession!"

Everyone exclaimed over the enchanting idea and rose to traverse to the beach. Urtzi took Esuvia's hand and more cheers went up. The small, rejoicing band traipsed through the pebbled sand and soon found themselves gazing in wonder at the sea waves that seemed to dance as joyfully as they to the shore.

"If my locket is received, it will not return unto me," Esuvia pondered aloud.

All watched in wonder as she hurled it into the waves. They stood for a long time gazing into the dark waters under the night sky, and the locket was not seen again. Esuvia noticed stars twinkling above the horizon, and she wondered if the locket had been accepted and become part of that expanse.

3

Find the River

Do nothing out of selfish ambition or vain conceit. Rather, in humility value others above yourselves. - Philippians 2:3 NIV

Urtzi and Esuvia embarked upon their pilgrimage one misty morning in early Junius to honour Juno, the goddess of marriage and childbirth. Urtzi carried tools in a backpack, as the plan was to walk during the brighter sunlit hours as far as they could past houses and settlements upon the road, and then to construct a raft for river travel. The couple aimed to camp by the river at night within a few feet of their raft that would be tied to a stake for quick release, lest wolves should threaten them. If the wolves pursued them by swimming, they would beat off the wolves with oars. Urtzi's insistence on these details seemed fueled by something between panic and fury, so Esuvia succumbed to the plan since the journey was to be one of unity and healing.

At first, Esuvia had suggested that they walk upon the Roman road from Dubris (Dover) to Durovernum (Canterbury) and remain upon the road until they arrived in Londinium. From Londinium, they could follow the River Tamesis (Thames) to the region where Urtzi claimed he had spent his childhood.

But Urtzi had other ideas. He wanted to walk around the coastline, on top of the cliffs, and in view of the sea from Dubris to the mouth of the Tamesis. He then wanted to steer a raft up the Tamesis to Londinium and beyond.

"Urtzi, that cannot be easily done," Tessera warned. "It could be dangerous to steer a small raft from the mouth of the Tamesis to Londinium. Is there no middle ground?"

"I must be within sight of the water," Urtzi insisted.

"Then walk along the shore and on the cliffs by the sea until you reach the mouth of the Tamesis. From there, walk along the shore by the river until you reach Londinium. If you fear the wolves, you can sleep by the shore of the Tamesis with your raft, should you need to escape to the water."

Urtzi's chin jutted forward as he pondered deeply, picturing with foreboding all that could transpire. Yet after a moment, he nodded slowly in agreement. Tessera slapped Urtzi's shoulder in a show of fatherly comradery, and though Urtzi could not smile, he let his jaw relax as he looked down at the ground and surrendered to the advice.

And so the trek began. Angi had advised deep conversation on the pilgrimage that was to be both spiritual and physical. The extended family present had adamantly agreed with her for Urtzi's and Esuvia's sakes. Physically, from the first steps of the journey the views were spectacular. Spiritually, the ensuing talks were to prove most life-giving and utterly essential.

They knew rustic farms were scattered atop the rocky ridges, with cattle and sheep grazing on the lime-rich grass. Urtzi and Esuvia were anticipating some level of hospitality from the human inhabitants. A steep path led up from Portus Dubris to the cliff tops, and it was with this climb that Urtzi and Esuvia began their journey.

The ocean wind was chilly for the month of Junius. It whipped Esuvia's ginger hair across her face and pushed back against the couple as they climbed with youthful strength up the path. For a moment, the power of the unexpected draft made Esuvia feel encased within a bubble of smallness and insignificance. She still felt quite alone walking behind Urtzi. He seemed lost within his own troubled thoughts and silence, but he turned at one particularly steep point and extended his hand to assist her. Then she felt a little warmer, as if perhaps she belonged somewhere in his world.

When they reached the top, she wanted to sink into the downy grass, wrap a shawl around herself, and tell Urtzi that the climb alone was all the journey that she needed. But the two of them put one foot forward, and then another, and then another, walking on in silence when bursts of wind made it difficult to chatter. The journey from Portus Dubris to Londinium was to be about a 66 mile walk, but would be significantly lengthened by Urtzi's determination to avoid parts of the Roman road.

The couple had been instructed to talk as they walked. They had always talked throughout their entire youth, but now Urtzi was lost in moments of the past. The pressure to bring it to the surface only distressed him more. Esuvia sensed this and intuitively tried to offer him extra support.

After they had walked about ten miles, the weather settled down, and Esuvia suggested some refreshment. "Let us rest for a while and take some food and drink," she encouraged Urtzi. He stopped walking and stood gazing off into the distance while waiting for Esuvia to present a spread.

She protested. "Urtzi, this pilgrimage is to encourage teamwork between us. Were we home and you were out building a boat, I would prepare a meal alone with gladness. But this is not the same."

Urtzi quickly moved to help her, and the first revelation from his past surfaced. "Esuvia, I did not grow up in a home with women. I do not know about such etiquette."

Esuvia paused and looked into his face to provide the space for him to elaborate.

He murmured, "You know neither of us had a mother or sister about."

"Yes, I know. We have compared that commonality several times." Esuvia remembered their many neighbourly talks around the dinner table in the evenings after work.

Urtzi worked to pull some lunch from a pack but kept glancing at Esuvia's face with darting eyes. She felt more was coming.

"That is why," he began, then stopped and clutched his stomach. "Oh ... I cannot speak about the weight of loss," his voice trailed away, and his secret remained buried.

Esuvia persisted. "There was no one else? You were completely alone for a very long time?"

Urtzi shook his head and moved to speak, but he was so panicked, he feared Esuvia could see his heart pounding through his tunic. He coughed and brushed the conversation aside with a wince on his face and jerky hand movements as he helped set out the lunch. After a moment, he answered, "It is true that I was alone for a very long time, but that is only part of the truth. I cannot talk about it right now." His voice was hoarse and trailed away in a rough whisper.

They sat down on a blanket and broke bread. Esuvia rubbed Urtzi's shoulder gently to reassure him. He seemed so distant suddenly that she was not sure he felt her touch. She had a sinking feeling that this was going to be a challenging journey indeed, and wondered if they would ever arrive.

***

The first night was far worse than the picnic. Urtzi dreamt of being surrounded by wolves. He woke up shouting. Esuvia reassured him that the wolves were necessarily hunted to keep them from the farms on the downs.

He then fell asleep and dreamt of hunting wolves. He awakened fantasizing about chasing the predators off of the cliffs with other hunters. Imagining flaming torches in hand, Esuvia walked with him in his fantasies to stare down at dozens of wolf bodies broken on the rocky beaches below the cliffs. They painted the adventure with story-telling, using the broad sky above as their canvas. Though it was a somewhat childish game, Esuvia began to feel Urtzi's hatred for the wolves even within her own heart.

***

The couple walked between ten and twenty miles each day. Esuvia constantly sought opportunities to draw forth Urtzi's story. The second dark night, the peaceful crackling of the small campfire they built together relaxed him and coaxed a piece of information from his tender heart sealed so tightly within his anxious chest.

"My brother and I told stories around the campfire."

Esuvia turned her face sharply toward Urtzi. She wanted to take a box and scoop the brother tale inside for safekeeping, yet she was afraid that some trust between them would shatter if she pushed too hard with words. So she said nothing and remained still.

"We lived beside the river. We owned a cart and we constructed a little hut. We fished and cooked on an open fire on the riverbank. We watched boats drift past. And I knew that someday I would build boats."

Esuvia sought about in her head for common ground to try to support him, but his beginning was so far away from what they had shared in their warm community in Portus Dubris. There, everyone loved the mosaic maker and the boy who built boats so industriously. The townspeople had shared joy over art and joy of working with the sun in their heads beside the spectacular cliffs rising over the bluest of seas. There had been no discussion of empty nights by dark rivers, so abandoned that only a hut sheltered him.

Suddenly Esuvia felt more troubled than ever that she had known so little about the man she agreed to marry. She pulled her shawl tighter around her shoulders and stared at the fire. She wondered if she would ever run away from this stranger. But now, he was taking her on a journey down a river path in her mind.

"We always kept the fire burning. All night, we had to wake to feed the flame because we lived in the woods, and the wolves were nearby. We knew the hut was not enough protection from them. We could barely lie down in the small frame. So we built a raft, oars, and a pole to move the raft in shallow waters, so we could escape if necessary. It is from that experience that I have resolved to construct a raft for our safety when we travel by the river."

Esuvia took a deep breath. Her heart was pounding. She was afraid of the woods surrounding the path that she and Urtzi traveled upon in their thoughts. She wanted to be in Portus Dubris again with everything as it had been before. Urtzi should be going out to build boats by the shore with trusted coworkers, and she should be walking in the sunlight to her father's workshop to create mosaics. Townspeople would be smiling and waving at the newlyweds while frying fish dinners emitted the pleasant aroma of herbs simmering in olive oil - a delicacy brought to the port by the merchant ships. The community would be reveling in their togetherness, enjoying the privileges life in a port city provided, as the scent of good food for the body and fellowship for the soul drifted abundantly among the dwellings. Urtzi and Esuvia should be home with their neighbours, not alone on a journey in the chilly dark, uncertain of where they were going.

"What are you expecting to find Urtzi? Is there anyone you know still living there near your childhood home?"

Urtzi closed his eyes against painful thoughts. He did not answer anymore and again Esuvia was left alone in the shadows, doubting any brightness would ever rise on a morning horizon.

***

And indeed, no bright summer sunrise greeted them on the morrow. They awakened to such heavy rain, they sought shelter. Some huts where shepherds lived were scattered upon the Downs. Urtzi and Esuvia did not hesitate to run to the first dwelling they happened upon during the deluge. They received a compassionate welcome to the rudimentary home and were extremely thankful to have a thatched roof over their heads.

A man, woman, and young child lived in the hut. The woman sat upon a bench, cradling the babe in a thin piece of cloth. The man stood, leaning heavily on a long walking stick. Their clothing was muddy, and their hair was pushed back with soured scarves. Their fingernails were black with dirt. But they were most kind. Natives to the region, they all spoke in a similar Brittonic tongue. They spread ragged sheepskins on the dirt floor and encouraged their guests to converse.

"What brought you all the way up here along the cliffs?" the man asked.

Esuvia looked at Urtzi politely, encouraging him to show household leadership. He took the cue. "We have just been wed. Our family has encouraged us to return to my childhood home to introduce my bride to ... my past ... the foundations of my life."

Urtzi and Esuvia smiled with strained expressions, realizing how different the privileges they had enjoyed in Portus Dubris were to the poverty of the shepherds' life experience. But the family before them embraced their humanity, understanding completely that a recently wedded couple needed to have bonding opportunities.

"Ah, we wish you great happiness!" the man exclaimed, and his wife smiled broadly with moist eyes. The host and hostess then locked eyes and, with mutual nods, she rose. While cradling the babe with one arm, she drew forth a rustic pot full of a hospitable beverage and poured it into clay cups.

"Pray for the blessing of the Roman god Junius on your marriage and the blessing of the Celtic goddess Erecura to give you children!" the man gestured with sweeping generosity.

The two couples cheerfully agreed with hope and thanksgiving, then drank from the cups.

"Did you grow up here on the Downs?" Esuvia attempted conversation.

They uttered affirmations with smiles from unassuming, humble faces. "We both learned to walk trailing behind the sheep herds!" the woman laughed.

Esuvia and Urtzi envisioned baby toddlers chasing after sheep and laughed too.

"Our baby will soon learn to walk the same way!" the mother added.

"What is your darling baby's name?" Esuvia began to glow with growing warmth for the sweet family.

"Her name is Aife (Beauty)," the new mother radiated joy.

"A glorious name!" exclaimed Esuvia. "And what are your names?"

"He is Cu (Hound), and I am Ness (Roaring One)."

"Did you grow up together hounding the sheep by dashing after them with loud voices?" Esuvia stabbed at some humour.

Cu and Ness exchanged a glance and then laughed again. "Oh, yes, we did so all the time!"

"Well, I am Esuvia (Beautiful, Radiant) and he is Urtzi (Sky)."

Cu and Ness looked blank. Neither name was familiar to them, as they were both of distant origins. The name Urtzi was Basque. Esuvia may have been Gaul or a Latinized name. Again, Esuvia felt the weird, uncomfortable feeling of having knowledge and experience that made her seem remote to these new friends.

Then Cu spoke up. "Well, the names Urtzi and Esuvia sound so beautiful together!"

"As do the names Cu and Ness!" Urtzi finally joined in.

Then the dark hut suddenly felt cozy, and the two couples began to wish that the heavy rain would last all day. And indeed, it did last for several hours. The new friends passed time exchanging folktales. Urtzi vaguely remembered tales from the Basque region told by his parents and grandparents. Cu and Ness knew shepherd's tales of lake people, and Esuvia knew tales of merpeople from her rearing by the sea. The storytelling enraptured the young adults with childish mirth. The little hut nearly glowed with unexpected joy.

When the rain stopped, the world seemed too sloppy for travel, and the new friends cast about for a way to manage a dry night together in the small hut. Finally, they worked out that each couple could camp near opposite walls of the room on shawls and sheepskins, waiting for a drier passage for their work and travel in the morning.

But when morning dawned, the two couples changed their plans.

Urtzi and Esuvia were drawn to helping Cu and Ness with their work and childcare. Cu and Ness were delighted to accept the offer from their new friends. Now the sun was glistening on the newly washed world around them. They all stepped out into the light and beamed with energy and refreshment.

"Let us help you gather in kindling and supplies. We can hold your baby for a while, as well, so you can catch up on some other chores," Esuvia suggested.

She cradled Aife while she followed Ness around as the young mother washed what she could and swept out the hut. Cu and Urtzi set out to herd the sheep to pasture and to search for firewood and fresh water supplies.

"We told our story of running behind the sheep together from toddler days!" laughed Ness. "Now it is your turn to tell your and Urtzi's story ... Su." She shortened Esuvia's name with friendly familiarity and glanced playfully at her as she hung laundry on a clothesline.

"Ah, yes! I agree!" laughed Esuvia. "I always called him 'the boy who walked out of the sea' because we lived in Portus Dubris by the sea, and none of us knew exactly where he came from. He actually did not come from the sea, though. He came from the river and spent his childhood inland. He is the second generation of immigrant grandparents. He cannot remember having ever lived anywhere else."

She paused and Ness nodded with understanding, watching Esuvia's face between clothesline pinnings to communicate genuine interest.

"Wherever he came from, he worked so hard. Everyone in town respected Urtzi. He is a boatbuilder."

She stopped. Her mind was ambling off on the path of how Urtzi acquired a house, but she knew better than to share anything about his possessions with one who had so little. Then she began a new direction.

"He would stop for supper with my father on the way home from his days of such hard work. He had no real family around. My mother died when I was born and an aunt in town stepped in to direct me when my father was at a loss as to how to raise a little girl."

Ness made an empathetic sound in her throat and looked at "Su" with softened eyes.

"Urtzi and I talked some about the loss of our mothers. He also teased me about my work. I helped my father with his work."

Again, she stopped. How could she tell an impoverished shepherd-ess about her privileged work as a respected mosaic artist?

But Ness was intensely interested in Esuvia's story, and stood watching her with large, innocent eyes. "What kind of work?" she urged "Su" to finish.

"Well ... uhm ... perhaps in some places it would be the work of slaves, but we ... my father and I ... are not slaves."

Ness's brows furrowed. "Go on."

"We ... work so hard. It is dusty, and my neck and back get so tired leaning over the ... the rocks."

"Are you a miner?"

"Oh ... no, not really. I mean, I gather seashells and pebbles on the beach if you want to call that mining!" Esuvia coughed a laugh nervously.

"Are you a fisherwoman?"

"Oh ... Ness, I am a ... a mosaic artist." Esuvia flushed and felt tears near the surface.

Ness studied her in silence for five seconds, but it seemed more like a dramatic twenty seconds, or perhaps sixty seconds. Then she said, "You make pictures for those fine Roman villas?"

"Yes, yes, that is what I help my father do!" Esuvia said loudly with a flood of relief at finally admitting her more privileged work.

Ness studied her for three more silent seconds and then said, "Was that hard for you to tell me because it is man's work and not woman's work?"

Esuvia nodded vigorously and protected her new friend with affirmative exclamations. "Yes, yes, I am so embarrassed that I do man's work! I hope you do not think less of me!"

Ness's kind eyes softened again. "Aw, Su, it's okay that you help your

Dad with his work. I don't think less of you. I bet you're good at it. He's lucky to have a daughter like you to help him."

Esuvia smiled and thanked her, and then, Ness said something else utterly unexpected. "So, are you going to help Urtzi build boats, now that you are married to him?"

Again, Esuvia sought about for the right words and found them. "Yes ... we will soon build a raft together to ride down the river to his childhood home."

Ness nodded and said seriously, "You be careful on the river. I want to see you both again on your return journey."

Esuvia suddenly felt her eyes welling up with emotion. She was not certain if it was the pure honesty of the sweet young shepherdess or the human need to begin building connections alongside Urtzi as a couple with a new life together, or both. Something was deeply touching about the moment. Esuvia turned away to hide her feelings and plucked a wildflower for baby Aife to enjoy.

***

The entire day on the Downs was blessed with pleasant exchanges of friendship for both the men and women. Ness and Su carried a basket of hard bread and dried apple slices out to the men at midday. Ness sheltered Aife in a sling. The tiny child slept peacefully against her mother's warmth in the breeze and sun. They all sat on shawls to eat in the grass littered with sheep dung.

Then Ness offered to teach Su to herd the sheep. Su agreed to run alongside Ness. So they frolicked through the wild grass under the early summer sky, singing ancient calls to the flock. Su lost herself in the sounds and senses of the experience. She began to believe that the day was eternal. She would run into the blue sky, and become one forever flying body with the wind, and the chase would never end.

At one point, she turned and caught a glimpse of Urtzi watching her with a pleased expression on his face. She turned back to the task Ness had given her, but her heart was suddenly pounding with the desire to live and embrace forever with her husband as her lover. She glanced over her shoulder at him again, and they exchanged a warm and gentle smile.

Suddenly, Esuvia was stopped short by the sight of a villa looming in the distance. She looked about for Ness, searching for an explanation. Ness moved alongside Esuvia and noted, "They own the herds we look after."

Now Esuvia realized that Ness was not entirely ignorant of human society. In fact, Ness was not ignorant in any way. Esuvia felt her face beginning to flush with shame over the ridiculous assumptions she had made about her new friend. Another veil slipped away. Esuvia looked at Ness and said without pretense, "I see."

Ness met her eyes with the same innocent expression, but now Esuvia could see the glint of wisdom there.

Another young woman moving across a paved walkway in the distance at the villa lifted a hand in greeting to Ness. Ness's face changed gently with appreciative recognition. "She is very kind," she murmured, and left Esuvia wondering whether the woman was a servant or an owner of the estate.

Esuvia decided not to ask. The spirit of the freeing experience she was having lent itself to not caring what anyone's social status was. She then found herself laughing as she and Ness returned to the hut to prepare some evening fare.

After sunset, all enjoyed a campfire roasting some wild hare and vegetables from Ness's small garden. As they had worked together all day, Cu had extracted some information from Urtzi about his fear of wolves. Now Cu took the hard line of telling legends of wolves to shake Urtzi from his deep awe and force him to face reality. Urtzi bore it all with newly found valor after a day spent clearing his head with the clifftop ocean breezes and the sheep's songs of joy for the grass.

Esuvia felt comforted as she fell asleep next to Urtzi in the hut for the second and final night at their new friends' abode. She and Urtzi had stepped away from the dark waters of a river of fear and glimpsed a better path sharing a river of kindness.

4

Cursed Water

When I was a child, I talked like a child, I thought like a child, I reasoned like a child. When I became a man, I put the ways of childhood behind me.
- I Corinthians 13:11 NIV

Urtzi and Esuvia rose in Britannia's bright summer dawn to continue their trek to Urtzi's childhood home by a river. Cu and Ness were already awake with baby Aife. The high energy of the new life and work ethic of the sheep herders was tangible in the tiny home. Esuvia felt as if it were the beginning of something new for her that only the understanding she had gained from them could have made possible. She followed closely behind Ness as they walked through the rickety, rotting door into the fresh world of flowing grass beyond.

The four young adults paused before parting ways. The beating heart of the new day could not pulse them forward any faster. Something very precious had passed between them as they shared their humanity so naturally, calmly offering one another support during the storm and workday that had followed.

They passed the darling baby Aife around the group one last time, reveling in the wonder of her childish worldview. Encircled by love, she glowed with joyful smiles and giggles, her strawberry blonde wisps tousled by the breezes blowing off the ocean and breaking on the cliff-sides. Last she came to Urtzi, and similar to the sinking feeling of the wedding day, Esuvia experienced shock at his response.

Urtzi's face contorted uncontrollably, and he nearly dropped Aife as he quickly handed her off to someone else. Esuvia sensed suddenly that he was about to lurch forward, and she grabbed his elbows tightly, one arm wrapped around his waist as she pulled his weight upward. There was a quick surge of anger in her grip and the force with which she nearly jerked him from pitching forward.

She bit her lip and flashed a quick, thin smile round the circle, but the weary look in her eyes betrayed her. Cu perceived the change and saved the moment.

"Something has happened," he instantly surmised. "Perhaps it is good, Esuvia. You are on a journey of discovery, and Urtzi's story is rising to the surface of his soul. If it did not come forth, your journey would be in vain."

Once again, Esuvia felt humbled by the raw intelligence of such true friends. She met Cu's eyes and slowly nodded. Her fierce grip on Urtzi gently changed to a caress of his bent back. He slowly relaxed.

"Urtzi, as you are walking today, you must tell Su why you felt so overwhelmed just now. Clearly something upset you. It is not for Cu and me to know, but you must share between the two of you what just disturbed you," Ness encouraged him.

Urtzi covered the lower part of his face with his hands and nodded. His gestures communicated that he was hiding something, but it would soon be shared. Cu and Ness nodded back to him and slowly reached out to gently hug him and Esuvia. Some tears welled in their eyes. And then, Urtzi and Esuvia moved away with sad glances over their shoulders and appreciative smiles.

Truth be told, it was so early in the morning, it was nearly the middle of the night. The sun was as bright as noonday at that time in the month of Junius in Britannia. The brightness had filtered through the roughly made walls of the hut beckoning to all to fling wide the door and run into the arms of the new day.

Now Urtzi and Esuvia were stepping through the grasses of the Downs, pushing their hair back from their eyes in the sea wind. Esuvia tried to let her cares be lifted away by the currents of air. The imagery helped, but she felt a tinge of irritation at Urtzi for his emotional collapse during their moment of departure. Perhaps they had arisen too early, and her own feelings were on edge due to the lack of rest. She tried to push the nagging thoughts aside and focus on the positivity of the new summer day and the intention of helping Urtzi rather than criticizing him.

He walked ahead of her and even his pace and very gait seemed to exude how lost in his own thoughts he truly was. Esuvia pulled some raisins from a pouch she had strapped across her shoulder and front of her tunic. She moved beside Urtzi and offered him a handful. He managed a half smile.

"So tell me, Urtzi, did the child remind you of your brother just now?"

Urtzi kept his eyes on the ground in front of him, but nodded. "Yes, I suppose holding the child stirred a memory." His mouth suddenly trembled.

"Urtzi - I am going to ask a sensitive question because it will help us in the long run to uncover this mystery. Did ... a wolf ... harm your brother?"

Urtzi forced his fingers through his thick wavy hair and exhaled his pent-up frustration. "No, a wolf did not harm my brother," he managed to confirm.

"Oh, that is good to hear. Thank you for letting me know," Esuvia gushed relief.

Urtzi interrupted her. "But ... he got very sick. And ... Su ... I hate wolves."

He quickened his pace, seeming to move away from Esuvia almost unintentionally, as if the memory of his brother's misfortune spurred him forward with blind rage.

She stopped and watched him charging on before she ran forward to resume the journey with him. She quickly caught up with him and feeling slightly sleep-deprived, she suddenly blurted out, "Urtzi, you cannot make me play guessing games! Please stop hiding the truth from me! It is utterly unfair to me in every way, " she gestured with her arms and hands for emphasis.

Urtzi worked his jaw, grinding his teeth. He stopped walking again and threw half of an explanation into the morning air. "My brother died very suddenly. He drank cursed water accidentally before I knew about the death within it. He died in my arms."

Then he was very angry that he had felt forced to remove the protective tomb he kept around the memory of his brother. His eyes flashed at Esuvia, and he stormed into the distance again.

This time, she walked a fair distance behind him, not attempting to catch him. They continued to walk with a long stretch between them for quite some time. The sun rose higher and the day grew even brighter. After about an hour, the charged emotions subsided, and the couple managed to reconnect.

As Esuvia walked by Urtzi's side, she softly apologised, "I should not have demanded an explanation in that way."

Urtzi shook his head slightly. "At some point, I had to tell the truth about the burden of my brother's death, though I wish we could have shared more gently. Never mind, the moment has passed."

Then they walked on in silence, side by side, for many miles.

The weather was fair, so when evening came, they agreed to sleep under the stars. Esuvia was surprised that Urtzi was willing to lie down in a field so far from the river, but the hours they had spent on the empty landscape had convinced them both that wolves were nowhere near. They agreed to attempt to take turns tending the fire and keeping watch, as the shepherds had described to them this alternative way of ensuring safety in the open wilderness.

The crackling fire and gentle night sounds calmed the feelings between them. "Let us put aside the goal of dredging up past sadnesses for a while, and remember the joy of our courtship," Esuvia suggested.

Urtzi's face lightened some. "Our courtship lasted many years. How long were we in love?"

Esuvia looked heavenward at the stars. "I do not remember a time when I was not in love with you," she said quietly.

Urtzi remembered seeing the slender, elegant figure bent over shells on the beach, her ginger hair catching the sun like fire. "I had never seen anyone so beautiful," he pondered.

He closed his eyes, remembering her smiling face looking up at him for the first time.

"I loved coming to the boatyard to watch you work," she said. Urtzi's strength and work ethic had always impressed her deeply.

"I loved watching your hands and eyes as you designed the mosaic templates," he said.

Suddenly she was beside him, and they embraced.

5

Pursued

... whither thou goest, I will go ... -Ruth 1:16 KJV

Urtzi and Esuvia finally reached Londinium on foot, as requested by Esuvia's father. As promised, they had walked from Portus Dubris (Dover) to nearly the mouth of the Tamesis (Thames) and turned westward on the banks toward the city. No wolves interfered.

Urtzi did awaken from another night of troubled sleep, having dreamt of something almost as terrifying as wolves. He had dreamt of nearly smothering under a great piece of fabric. When he awakened from the nightmare, he pondered for many hours how his awful memories had begun to surface when the tablecloth came floating down through the air at his wedding ceremony. After dwelling on his thoughts for many dark hours of the night, the sun rose, and Urtzi resolved to speak with Esuvia.

"My love ... " he caressed her cheek to gently stir her from her light dawn sleep. Her eyes fluttered open. Urtzi moved his face close to hers.

"I must apologise, Esuvia." He looked very solemn. "I am sorry that I kept a part of myself hidden from you. I did not mean to cause you any harm. I did not realise that such awful memories would pursue me into my future life with you."

Esuvia smiled slightly. "I understand, Urtzi. I know you did not realise that anything was wrong with trying to put the past behind you. You did not intend to leave me out, only to protect me and proceed positively. I forgive you, if there is anything to forgive. I know you did not expect the memories to come charging after you like wolves trying to tear you to pieces."

Urtzi's eyes darkened and he sat up suddenly. Esuvia sighed shortly and leaned up on her elbow. "What on earth is it this time?" her voice was edged with irritation.

Urtzi shook his head and pulled his hands over his ears, moaning, "Oh, Su. The wolves were not metaphorical. There were real wolves in my life."

Esuvia reached for his shoulder, trying to be more gentle. "I know you always had to keep your campfire burning and a raft staked beside your hut because yes, there were real wolves."

Urtzi suddenly shot to his feet. "Let us explore Londinium today," he changed the subject.

Esuvia shot to her feet too. "No, Urtzi. If there is more for you to tell me, I will go no further on this journey with you until I know what is still pursuing us."

Beads of perspiration were forming on Urtzi's brow and lip. He began shoving his belongings into his backpack. Finally, he paused and took Esuvia's shoulders, squarely facing her.

"Esuvia, I promise you that I will tell you everything before we reach the riverbank where I spent my childhood. Just as so much has already been shared through this journey, we will complete it, and all will be told."

Esuvia looked deeply into his eyes. "You promise, Urtzi," she said quietly.

Urtzi nodded with definite intention and said with strength, "I promise you, Esuvia."

Satisfied, she too began to pack and soon, they were nearing the city dwellings. The Tamesis River Valley stretched green and fertile as far as the eye could see. Of beautiful, pale limestone and red tile roofs,

Londinium nestled compactly and with glorious Roman order on the shores. A bridge spanned the view.

Esuvia took a deep breath to curb the nervous feelings jittering in her heart and stomach. Urtzi showed no emotion and said simply, "We do not need to walk straight into all of that. We can bypass the city and continue on the river, if we choose. Is there any need at all for us to enter the city?"

Esuvia slowly shook her head. "No, I truly cannot think of anything unless we want to buy some food. I just do not know where we would go to find a market."

Urtzi squinted in thought. "We could lose ourselves in the crowd looking for a food stall and perhaps seem inconspicuous."

Esuvia looked down at her dirty tunic in which she had slept and hiked for days on end. "I look disheveled. I might attract attention."

Urtzi agreed that he too looked unkempt. "We might bypass the city and find a farmhouse selling food on the outer limits beyond. A farmer might not demand a cosmopolitan appearance from us."

Esuvia nodded. "That is not implausible."

So they set out to walk around the perimeter of the great town.

As they enjoyed the convenience of roads, Esuvia pondered, "Do we wish to continue as we began? Shall we truly travel by the river? Could we not journey by road?"

Urtzi could not shift his thinking. "No, I do not know the way by road. The river will take us to my home. But we must find a place to construct a raft, or buy one."

Esuvia felt wearied by the suggestion, but she trusted Urtzi's building skills.

They reached the western limits of Londinium and as hoped, farm houses were not far away. It was not long before they located a seller of produce and sought advice about rafts and materials for building. The seller pointed them to another farm on the road within two miles. That farmer also fished on the nearby river and owned some small vessels.

* * * * *

Maglocunos (name meaning "king of the hounds") owned a well-developed farm including livestock, grain, fishing vessels, and hunting tools. He was a formidable man with a dark visage, and among his hunting tools, were fierce dogs. It was rumoured that Maglocunos even trained dogs of war for the Roman army. The charcoal grey thunder-heads hanging over his reputation deeply veiled his financial pursuits.

The sounds of the dogs rebounded over the empty rural landscape. Howls and low-pitched voices of the powerful canines Maglocunos employed in his service rang across the river and stilled the wind. Upon this unexpected cacophony of the army of eager, aggressive hounds rooting endlessly behind the walls, longing to leap at prey, came gentle, timid Urtzi and Esuvia.

"This ... this cannot be the farm that was recommended?" Urtzi stammered when they were half a mile away and heard the disturbing din.

"Let us bypass this place at once, Urtzi. I would rather go hungry and walk in lost circles until my feet bleed than approach this fear-haunted place," Esuvia gasped.

But no sooner had her exclamation left her lips than the hooves of a horse approached behind the vulnerable couple on foot. The two defenseless humans turned round and followed their gaze upward to the grey face of a tall man with long, black locks of hair, sitting high upon a rippling-muscled steed.

Speechless, Urtzi and Esuvia could not divert their eyes from the "king of the hounds". Arrogant and intentionally intimidating, Maglocunos turned his horse in proud circles as he leered down at the helpless couple before him. A loveless man, their unified presence annoyed him, and he instantly began to work an angle in his mind as to how he could harass and punish them.

"Why are you trespassing on my property?" he taunted them, though they were not truly very near his actual land.

"We are following the river, only bypassing your estate," Esuvia blurted out, all too keenly aware of Urtzi's terror of all things Lupus and Canis.

Maglocunos scoffed immediately at Urtzi. "Are you a woman? Why do you let this girl speak for you?"

Esuvia glanced at Urtzi and began to panic. Her body became very stiff and her feet moved back and forth as she sought about for what to do while holding her tongue.

Urtzi could think of nothing to deter the maleficence of the powerful king of dogs other than to act submissive, like a dog. So he suddenly feigned an interest in the pack and said, "Do your dogs kill wolves?"

Maglocunos's eyes glittered at Urtzi's unexpected response to provocation. Playing with his prey, Maglocunos bantered, "Oh, yes. There are hardly any wolves to be found in these lands because my dog packs have killed them all. But if you wish to be a wolf-killer, I will take you on a hunt." He sized the medium-sized Urtzi up with a cruel glance.

Fearing for Urtzi's life, Esuvia moved to stop him from engaging further. Afraid to speak for him again, she touched his arm and implored him with her eyes. But Urtzi had already been hooked by the evil huntsman.

A pagan young man, Urtzi thought the sudden change in events might be a gift from the gods to fulfill his dreams of breaking wolves to pieces. Many nights had been spent running through fields of dreams with flaming torches and spears, shouting and herding wolf packs over the sea cliffs. Now perhaps he had met a leader he was always meant to meet. Surely the gods had led him here.

Esuvia's light touch became a firm grip, and Maglocunos saw and hated them more. Esuvia pleaded, "Please, gentlemen, we only wish to follow the river to my husband's childhood home. Please allow us to simply pass in peace."

His senses heightened by the male aggression of both men and dogs, Urtzi jerked his arm away from his wife. "I would very much like to hunt any wolves troubling these lands."

Maglocunos sneered at Urtzi's attempt to cover his raw aggression with statements of noble intention. The hunt was now unstoppable. Maglocunos's hatred of the innocence of the united couple and Urtzi's seemingly senseless hatred of wolves would drive the killing forward. Esuvia could feel tears streaming unbidden down her face.

"Meet me within the walls. I will ride ahead of you, and my slaves will open the gates," Maglocunos commanded. The horse's hooves splattered mud on Urtzi and Esuvia as he charged away.

Esuvia began to sob. "Urtzi, stop it! Stop it! Ten minutes ago, we were walking along a river in peace looking for simple raft materials and raw fruit. Now you have become instantly possessed by a dark power! What am I to do? I will run away! I will run away!" She sank into the muddy road.

On her knees in the sludge, Esuvia continued to rant, "You should have told me that you were possessed by a wolf demon! That is it, isn't it? You have been worshipping wolves! This demonic half-man of the blackest night has appeared out of your dreams and driven your madness into the open!" She stood again and began pacing back and forth, unseeing, unhearing, unfeeling anything but an all-consuming fear.

Urtzi stood and watched her for a few empty moments, then charged ahead. She wailed after him,"Urtzi! Where am I to go? What am I to do? I will be thrown to that monster's dogs! We are the prey! Can you hear them? Their sounds are terrible! They are fierce creatures, made malicious by a man who has lost his humanity! We have stumbled upon insanity! Please desist! Please desist!"

But everything within him was telling Urtzi that his entire life had led up to this point. Nothing could stop him. He was pulled forward by a wicked force that knew his weakness and sought to devour him.

Esuvia ran after him, crying out, "You mean nothing to that man, Urtzi! He wants to destroy you for no reason! He is a hunter of any game, including people weaker than himself! He will forget you when you are strewn upon the ground as broken meat for dogs, and I will be left alone to die! We have a peaceful life, Urtzi! Let us return to our peaceful life!"

At this, Urtzi spun on his heel and marched directly back to Esuvia. He grabbed her shoulders and stared hard into her eyes, "I have no peace!" he uttered with a sound that seemed to come from a hollowness as empty, dark, and devoid of life as hell itself.

Esuvia began to wail. "You promised me, Urtzi! You promised me only a little while ago that you would tell me why you hate the wolves! You promised to complete our journey! But if you do this, we will both die here for no reason other than the sport of a cruel man who exchanged his soul for that of a hound of hell!"

"No - this is part of our journey! I will finish this! I will ride with the dogs and kill the wolves!" Urtzi shouted.

"Urtzi, you know me! You do not know that man! He sees you as game for his dogs! Powerful Roman generals will pay him for his dogs of war after we are dead, and the blood-thirsty devils will only kill more people! Why should we give our lives for this?"

Urtzi suddenly held her face between his hands and said with certainty, "We will not!" and then stormed away toward the walls.

Esuvia sank in the mud again, weeping. "We will! We will die here!" And for a while, she despaired. Then, as the sun sank in the sky, casting its reflection over the rippling river, she rose and with resolve moved toward the walls to die with Urtzi. If they were to be killed for their innocence and love, then they would die together.

6

The Turn in the Woods

... may ruin overtake them by surprise-may the net they hid entangle them, may they fall into the pit, to their ruin. - Psalm 35:8 NIV

Through the dark night, they rode. Maglocunos had selected two slaves to ride with him and Urtzi. The slaves had been prisoners of war and were traded in a shady deal by a Roman officer in exchange for dogs of war. The two men were skilled riders and huntsmen, but Maglocunos treated them as a material presence rather than human. He always looked past them, never making eye contact. Occasionally, they would glance at Urtzi, and he tried to maintain a neutral but non-threatening expression. He wondered if they knew that he could feel empathy for them.

Urtzi had learned to ride horses from Adrian, the house owner he had assisted before he became the heir. Adrian kept two horses for transport. In the evenings after working at the boatyard, Urtzi would exercise Adrian's horses on the beach and wait for them to graze in a pasture until dusk. Many beautiful evening hours were spent with Esuvia assisting with the horses' care.

Now Urtzi kept remembering Esuvia's words that he was the prey. Perhaps this was not an outing of pleasant sportsmanship like those

Adrian shared with Urtzi, and Urtzi then shared with Esuvia. But the Maglocunos hunting party had heard howling in the distant forest areas, so Urtzi doubted that it was true that he was prey. He felt pulled toward the howling wolves.

Maglocunos rode proudly ahead as if he were a Roman general. It was true that he did not seem human. He rather exuded a determination not to reflect any humanity. His only purpose in life was to hunt, kill, and dominate.

The hunting party was tense, feeling doomed by the lack of camaraderie and singular purpose. Urtzi would never have known what it meant to be on a team if he had not bonded through work with the boatbuilders in the shipyard. His only memory of early companionship was the brother he cared for after his parents died. He remembered very little about being nurtured by his family. He had appreciated the connections that friends such as Esuvia and her father had given him in Portus Dubris over evening meals. The fellowship around their table had been a warm light in his life of shadows.

Perhaps the lack of experience was why he now found himself riding behind a half-man, half-monster with whipping black hair and piercing, hateful coals for eyes. Urtzi had never known true hatred except for his malice toward wolves. He knew mostly loneliness. Perhaps that emptiness within his past left him vulnerable to the danger that should have been glaringly obvious emanating to him from Maglocunos.

Though he seemed possessed, Urtzi was truly obsessed with a need to avenge love. Perhaps it was this one characteristic of his strange pursuit that shielded him somewhat. There was light within him. Within Maglocunos, there was neither love nor light.

On they rode through the darkness, sometimes quickly, sometimes stealthily. The highly trained dogs ran in silence and with intensity to find and rend their prey to pieces. Finally, the forest grew quiet, and a certainty that the wolves were near and aware of their presence enveloped the four riders. Though on horses, Urtzi feared being surrounded by wolves. The hunting party high on their steeds and protected by dogs would have the advantage even if that were to happen, but Urtzi's heart was pounding hard enough to kill him.

He thought of Esuvia. He should have told her why he hated the wolves so that she would understand the risk he took to destroy them. She could never have completely understood, but if he had offered her his explanation, she would have not been left alone in such bewilderment.

Urtzi was no true hunter. He was neither fierce, nor even much of a survivalist. He had been drawn to the work of boatbuilding, and to this he had applied himself. But it was his ability to connect with people that had won a place for him in the community in Portus Dubris.

But tonight, Urtzi was determined to wield a savage hunt and kill the wolves. He let his hatred for them well up and consume any feelings of mercy within him.

Suddenly, Maglocunos held up his hand to signal that the wolves were near. In his dreams, Urtzi had pursued the beasts with torches until they sailed down over the edges of cliffs by the hundreds. But there were no torches on this dark night. The moon and stars were covered by thick clouds.

There is a feeling sometimes described of pending death. This indefinable and yet certain awareness began to creep over Urtzi, and he realized it was a premonition of his own death that he was sensing. He had seldom prayed to any gods, and certainly not to a wolf god as he had been accused of by Esuvia. But at that moment, he began to wish that he could pray to any god that would hear him.

Maglocunos turned to him with chilling eyes, and Urtzi then knew that the wild wolves had long since fled from the horses and dogs they most certainly knew were approaching. For what felt like an endless stretch of time and heartbeats, the psychopath held Urtzi with his icy gaze. Though terrified, Urtzi faced Maglocunos with an expressionless face, knowing nothing else to do but to avoid provoking more sick pleasure with fear.

To lengthen the emotional torture, Maglocunos paced with his horse a few steps back and forth, mocking Urtzi with his awesome power over the utterly helpless. Urtzi's head began to swim with his pounding pulse, and his vision became blurry. The killer dogs growled ferociously in their throats and bared their awful teeth. The slaves, the horses, and the dogs had surrounded him and were coldly focused on his destruction. Then Urtzi knew the moment had come.

What happened next could never be recounted clearly by him. Urtzi may have begun to faint and lost a moment of time. But when Maglocunos gave a nod to his slaves and dogs to attack Urtzi, the slaves and dogs turned and attacked the cruel master instead.

The unexpected turn of events shocked Maglocunos, and he faltered. In that state of confusion, he was easily knocked from his horse. He began to fight, swinging a knife while holding his ground on his feet. In the furious flurry, Urtzi spied from his peripheral vision a woman charging from the dark trees, bareback on a mare. She courageously leapt down and hurled a heavy rock into the violent fray at Maglocunos's shoulders. He fell to the ground. Then, Urtzi swept Esuvia up onto his steed, and they fled for their lives, leaving Maglocunos to face the future he had chosen for himself through his evil pursuits.

They never looked back. And wild dogs remained on that isle for 1,000 years!

7

Enwrapped

Brothers and sisters, we do not want you to be uninformed about those who sleep in death, so that you do not grieve like the rest of mankind, who have no hope. - I Thessalonians 4:13 NIV

They rode on without stopping until afternoon of the next day. They had eventually found their way back to the river. They did not speak even to discuss the question of from whence came the mare Esuvia rode on the rescue mission. Their silence ensued until the noon hour had passed, and both had the same thought that they would rather dismount, eat, and rest in the bright daylight. Esuvia quietly revealed that she took the horse from a stable outside the walls of the house grounds. There it had been neighing and kicking its stall loudly in fear of the sounds of the horrible dogs.

Their emotions were completely spent. They felt nothing of anger or sorrow, only exhaustion and a kind of blankness - perhaps a state of shock.

"Maglocunos is surely dead or lying badly wounded alone in the woods," Urtzi finally uttered quietly as they ate hard bread while sitting on a fallen log by water's edge. "The slaves would have had no alternative but to defend themselves and flee."

Esuvia shook her head in disbelief at all that had transpired. She could find no words for the situation. She could only breathe, and eat, and stare around her, first at the ground, then into the distance.

"The dogs probably returned to the house," Urtzi surmised. "Any other slaves and servants would realize that something was wrong." He paused. "It is hard to believe anyone would try to rescue him, though. Perhaps many more prisoners escaped when he did not return."

Esuvia roused from her state of reverie. "I wonder if there were others involved in a planned escape. Perhaps they all knew that the predator was about to become the prey."

Urtzi sighed shortly. "A part of me doubts that he is dead. It is difficult to kill a monster."

Esuvia shuddered. "How does anyone become like him?"

Then, they were silent again and pondered many questions about the state of humankind and their own souls. They swung between relief and guilt, and were perplexed. Once, Urtzi spoke so quietly, his voice was nearly a whisper. "I truly wanted to hunt wolves to save human life. And then, you saved my life."

Esuvia could not smile, but her face relaxed some. "Oh no, I only knocked the man down so that you could run away with me."

Then, they were quiet some more. Finally, Esuvia approached the inevitable question she had for her husband. "Wolves usually only attack sheep and other livestock, but seldom attack human beings. Is that correct?"

Urtzi's jaw worked hard and his eyes narrowed. He blocked her passage to his thoughts with an aside, "Well, if that is so, killing wolves saves human life in an indirect way. If they eat our livelihood, we should do something to protect our food."

Esuvia sighed, too exhausted to poke around for more information. After they had finished their bread, she said quietly, "Let us please ride further. Let us ride as far as the horse can safely take us."

Urtzi nodded with strong agreement, and they mounted the horse again. That evening, they built a bonfire so big it blocked their fears. At least it was comforting to think no wolf would come near that fire, and a wounded or dead Maglocunos was many miles away. Staring at the light, they drifted into a dreamless sleep.

Near dawn, they heard the sound of wheels on stone and realized that their river path was near a road at this point. They both bolted up, staring wide-eyed around them until they regained a memory of their location and all that had transpired.

Urtzi bravely whispered that he would check to see if the cart or chariot was connected to Maglocunos. He crept through brush and shrubbery and peered through at the road.

The passing vehicle was disappearing into the distance, but Urtzi could make out a small family of passengers. With no time to consult Esuvia, he felt an urgency to appeal to safety in numbers and broke through the brush to call to them. After a moment, they slowed to a stop and turned to see why they were being summoned.

Urtzi's wave was on a spectrum between friendly and frantic. He jogged toward them and tried to force a smile on his tired, dirty face. They patiently waited for an explanation.

"We are camping by the river. Many miles behind us and nearly two days ago, we ran into trouble at a farm where a man raises dangerous dogs. We just awakened to the sound of your family passing on the road and decided to see if it might be better to travel behind you for safety. We have a horse."

The man and his wife looked openly at one another and willingly agreed. A hooded child sat between them. Her head was bent down in sleep, so Urtzi could not make out her face. The man was a fair, middle-aged Celtic man, and his wife was very young. They waited peacefully in the morning sun. Urtzi and Esuvia cleared their campsite then rode forth on the horse they had acquired from the death hunt deviously arranged by Maglocunos.

The young woman smiled warmly at Esuvia with a pleased expression before the man clicked his tongue at the little mule pulling his cart, and the entourage moved forward. Esuvia noted that there was a confident air of tranquility about the family. They rode in the calm quiet to only the sound of twittering birds and the stirring of gentle breezes for one to two hours.

At midday, it grew warm and the travelers stopped to water their horses and remove their wraps. The hooded child had not awakened until she was pulled up and the fabric pushed back from her face. Whitish-blonde curls matted against her rosy cheeks and forehead were then revealed. Her mother brushed her hair with her fingers, cooing and comforting the little girl.

Esuvia moved to fuss over the beautiful little girl but stopped short when she saw that Urtzi was frozen, staring at the mother and child. Esuvia had languished so many weeks now over the unforeseen strangeness of her new husband, and she once again felt like forcefully jerking him from his inwardly focused thoughts. "Are you alright?" she spoke sharply, trying not to clench her fists.

Urtzi was brought up short. "Oh, I apologise. Your daughter looks familiar to me," he said, then turned away to remove some items from his pack.

"What is the matter with you?" Esuvia whispered, feeling irritation rising at his lack of self-awareness.

"I said she reminded me of someone."

"Then who would that be? I am so sick of your secrets that cause such strong reactions to everyone you meet!" Esuvia berated him.

Urtzi shook his head. "I will tell you at a more appropriate time."

"And when will there be a more appropriate time?" Esuvia demanded.

At that moment, the gentle father walked around the horse behind which they were arguing. "We would like to share our fare with you as your journey has evidently been more difficult than ours," he offered. "My dear wife packed plenty of food. Please come and sit together with us on our shawls, and refresh your bodies and souls with a meal."

Urtzi and Esuvia lowered their eyes, feeling ashamed, yet they agreed.

Soon they were communing over lunch in the pleasant summer air. They broke bread and passed sauces in clay pots around for dipping. Dried fruits, cheese, nuts, and weak wine were among the filling options. Jerky and dried fish also came out of the basket that the wife had laid in the flat bed of the cart they pulled.

They seemed to have some authoritative knowledge about the road upon which they traveled, so Urtzi began asking questions. "Does this road follow the river very far?" he queried.

"Oh yes, the road never strays far from the Tamesis. The Romans frequently transfer goods from rafts to carts upon the road. You can always find the river nearby."

Urtzi looked around him carefully and thought that the region was beginning to look familiar to him.

"Might we ask where you are going?" Esuvia wondered curiously.

"Oh, we are on a journey to see family members. We have not been in this region since before our daughter was born. My wife was ill after the birth and is only now able to travel. Our daughter is four years old." He paused then asked, "And you?"

Esuvia looked at Urtzi, encouraging his leadership and social skills. Urtzi responded, "Yes ... we have only just married ... perhaps ... four or five weeks ago. We were advised by a mentor to make a journey to my childhood home. Though we have known one another for many years, there are so many new things to discover."

Esuvia remained silent, allowing the meal to bring restoration to her spirit.

"Might we ask your names?" the woman kindly appealed.

"Yes, certainly. I am Urtzi. My name is from the Basque mountain region far from here, but I was born nearby. My wife is Esuvia, and she is from Portus Dubris."

Smiles and murmurs were shared encouragingly. "And you?" Esuvia managed, beginning to recover her emotional strength again.

The woman answered. "My name is Aidna, and this is my husband Angus. Our daughter is named Aurora Christina. Her first name is after her aunt, Angus's sister who passed many years ago. Her second name is after her aunt's child - Tina - an elder cousin of whose fortune we are seeking to inquire on this journey."

"Oh, and how much further must you journey to find her locality?" asked Esuvia.

"Only a day further, I should think," Angus answered. His brow furrowed then because he noticed that Urtzi was running his hands nervously through his hair quite rapidly. But Angus said nothing.

They finished their meal a few minutes later and decided to travel further before evening. The lazy summer afternoon was passed in silence only broken by the hooves of the horses and the wheels of the cart. The ladies dozed gently.

Around the evening campfire, they again discussed the relative they were seeking. Urtzi had once more seemed preoccupied for most of the day and only became involved in the conversation about the aunt of Christina.

"So, you have not heard from your relative in four years?" Esuvia asked.

"Unfortunately, I have not heard from her, my niece. Aidna was extremely ill and nearly died. I could think of nothing but caring for our daughter and saving the life of her mother."

"You know ... I was the orphaned grandson of immigrants," Urtzi suddenly shared. Esuvia stared at him sharply, but tried to quell her judgements to hear him out. "I lived in a fisherman's hut by the river raising my brother after my parents died from the plague. I wonder if your sister was as poor as I, or perhaps she was a farmer, or a shepherdess ... " his voice trailed away with questions hanging in the evening air.

Angus looked slightly uncomfortable yet answered truthfully. "No, I am only a merchant from Londinium, but my niece is the heiress of a Roman villa. Her parents also died. When I last saw her, she was living on the villa with an extraneous heir named Julius who was selected to raise and care for Tina."

Urtzi's eyes began to dart about. Esuvia watched his face, her chest heaving with frustration over his secrets and how strangely he behaved as a result. Then she saw tears trickle down his cheeks. Unbidden, tears also began streaming from her eyes.

Angus and Aidna were suddenly aware and deeply concerned by the dramatic shift in the mood of the campfire setting. Aidna instinctively moved to place an arm around Esuvia's shoulders to stop the shaking. The awful hiddenness of the journey into the unknown had reached an impasse. The head of a volcano was about to explode into the atmosphere, and they were all suddenly quaking.

Urtzi could not control his voice as he roughly blurted the question, "Did Tina look like her father's side of the family? Long, fair curls?"

Angus's face clouded. "Yes, our child Christina looks exactly like my sister Aurora and her daughter - my niece also named Tina."

Urtzi covered his face with his hands and began to sob deeply, groaning. Everyone, including the child who did not understand what was happening, began to struggle, tearing up over his distress. Finally, Urtzi cried with broken voice, "I think I know who Tina is!"

Angus was clearly emotional but nodded cautiously. "Go on, man. You must tell us."

Urtzi stood and paced around the fire, wringing his hands. "Tina, you say. We called her Pura (Pure). Sometimes we also called her Pura Lux (Pure Light). She brought us loaves of bread wrapped in shawls throughout the plague. My little brother would run to the rock table between the woods by the river and the sheep fields to collect her offerings. I am sorry, Esuvia, but I could not bear it when your Aunt Priscilla brought me bread wrapped in shawls!"

Esuvia remembered the scene at Urtzi's house with him writhing in bed and collapsing further into grief when Priscilla reached out to him with her gift of bread wrapped in a shawl.

Urtzi covered his face with his hands and cried some more. Everyone cried.

"Our parents had died. Our Pura - your Tina was the mother the gods gave to us to feed us with warm bread and her concern. We knew she saw us." He paused and his face crumpled as he said again, "She saw us. We felt we were not completely alone."

Angus nodded wisely. "Thank you. Though painful, your news is comforting. Whatever happened to her, her life was not in vain. You are alive."

Urtzi hung his head. The group grew silent. Angus then knew from the silence and the mournful stance that Urtzi knew more than he had yet shared. The silence grew heavier. Tears stopped flowing and the group held their breath.

"One day, my brother drank water from the river before we saw that dead animals were floating in it. The water flowed past ahead of the floating animals, and he drank it unknowingly. A few weeks later, he died in my arms."

Utterances of condolence were softly spoken. Then Urtzi found the strength to finish his tale. "It was that kind of death that made the awful thing I later witnessed ... the tragic scene of horror ... so unbearable," he shuddered, then went on. "One evening, I heard singing floating on the evening air, so I emerged from the woods to see our Pura ... Tina ... cradling a lamb. Then, in a flash, a mother wolf attacked to tear the lamb away from her!"

Angus groaned and sank to the ground. Aidna ran to him, and Esuvia flew to Urtzi.

"I would have run to help her, but suddenly, another man came running from the road to her! He was shouting and screaming! I had seen him before, helping with the sheep shearing and the planting the previous spring. He kept wailing at the sky and calling out! The sounds he made ... it was so terrible! I could not move or interfere. It went on and on, and then he wrapped her in cloths - perhaps an ornate tablecloth - and carried her body back to the villa." Urtzi paused, then uttered one last agonizing cry, "I do not know for certain, but I think she may have died in his arms ... just as my brother had died in my arms!"

Esuvia began to sob with both grief and relief that his story was finally told. She wrapped her arms around him and held him for a very long time. The group remained by the fire consoling one another until the embers disintegrated to grey ash, and the night enwrapped them all in black velvet drapes, both comforting for the living and symbolic of the sleep of death.

8

To Cry and Live Till I Die for All the Joy and Pain

For you formed my inward parts; you knitted me together in my mother's womb. - Psalm 139: 13 ESV

The heaviness of their eyes and heads from the sadness of the night of crying made them think that they would never recover from the tragic news. No one spoke as they boiled porridge and checked the horse's hooves, except that Angus noted that he kept hearing carts passing during the night. "Perhaps the sojourners are trying to avoid detection by the Roman authorities," he pondered.

Aidna tried to smile cheerfully at her daughter who kept peering round at the group of adults with keen little observant eyes. Angus remembered his sister Aurora making a crown of wildflowers for little Tina so many years ago. Now he tried to imitate her, and Christina vowed to wear the crown all day.

The families had agreed that, though it would be difficult to approach a potentially deserted villa where the death of a loved one might hang over the land, it would be best to complete the journey and verify as much of the actual history as they possibly could. Their tear-wells had dried up, so many tears had been spent. All that they could do was face the day with courage, though their hearts felt like bricks, and their breathing was uneasy.

The wheels of the cart inched forward under a grey sky. With beautiful heads held high, the horses accepted the challenge of transporting the people to their destination. Little Christina leaned on Aidna's arm feeling the cloudy emotions of the group after the unsettling news. No one dared to hope for anything but closure to the story of Tina's death.

Urtzi wondered if the sleepless night of weeping had caused Esuvia to feel sick. She asked him to stop the horse once and ran into the woods to vomit. When she returned, he studied her carefully as she mounted the horse. Her cheeks were so pallid and her eyes so tired.

By the time the party paused for lunch, Urtzi was seized with a growing fear. He wanted to ask Esuvia if it were true but did not want to agitate her any more than he had already done on the long journey. He kept glancing at her nervously, his fears so much bigger than his hopes. All he wanted was her. All he wanted was for someone in his life to stay with him forever.

He noticed that she would not look at him. He knew she knew that he knew. They could not handle any more drama, so they avoided the subject. No one would notice their silence in the already deafeningly silent group.

Then they moved on again. Now he was noticing the attentiveness of the father to his child in the cart ahead of him. Now he was remembering Cu, Ness, and their baby. Now he was picturing the first night that he and Esuvia had been unafraid to sleep under the open sky on the Downs. He swallowed hard. He all but stopped the horse.

Esuvia read his thoughts and reprimanded him. "Urtzi, if you throw up, I will fistfight you."

Now he recalled her many jibes. She had called him a merman, plates had been thrown at his door when he was sick, and she had forced him to cook upon the road. Stormy, dark-eyed, hot-headed Su with her glorious hair of fire had jerked him back to reality so many countless times with her sharp tongue and her firm arm grips. And then, she had saved his life with more strength than a man when she hurled a stone at Maglocunos's shoulder blades and knocked him off his feet. Now, he glanced down and saw her small, white hands around his waist and he wanted to protect her so much, his heart was in his throat.

He held the reins with one hand for a moment and gently placed his free hand down upon hers. He could almost hear her thinking what to do next, and then he felt her lean her head against his back. And all at the same time, he wanted to cry and live till he died for all the joy and pain that life can hold.

9

Message from a Pendant

The people that walked in darkness have seen a great light: they that dwell in the land of the shadow of death, upon them hath the light shined.
- Isaiah 9:2-7 KJV

They did not reach the villa that day, as hoped. They knew that they were very close, but dusk came on, and they had to pause. "Who are these people who keep passing in the dark?" Angus and Aidna asked once again as another cart passed after they had stopped for the night. Angus actually got up and ran near the road to observe when more carts crept past.

While eating some supper around the campfire, Aidna leaned over to spoon some food from a cooking pot, and Esuvia noticed her necklace dangling. It stood out to Esuvia because she had thrown her own locket into the sea when her family had marched to the beach with the healer, Angi. Esuvia had believed that if the locket did not return to her, her offering was accepted by the sea gods and was perhaps transported to the stars. Why did Aidna wear a necklace?

Aidna felt Esuvia's weary stare. Inhibitions had fallen away as the reality of life had set in with such force on the journey. Aidna reached for the pendant instinctively and smiled at Esuvia. Then Aidna remembered that Tina had given it to her, and unable to bear more weeping, she swallowed and sat down hard with determination. She scooped her food in a hurry to force it down along with the lump in her throat.

Esuvia stared a while longer, then willed herself to tear her eyes away from the questionable object. She wanted to know, but she felt that Aidna did not want to be asked.

Nevertheless, after a few minutes, Aidna felt that she should explain. It was an opportunity to open the door to a discussion about faith. So she explained what the fish pendant on the necklace meant.

Now Urtzi and Esuvia sat dumbfounded. Everyone knew that the Christians had caused the plague by angering the gods. Why would anyone celebrate something, even wearing paraphernalia representing a belief that had resulted in so much suffering? In fact, none of this would even be happening, and all of their lives would be different, if only the gods had not been angered when Christians embraced exclusive faith.

Suddenly, Angus laughed out loud. No one else moved. His laughter sounded so strange after the night and the day spent mourning the terrible tragedy.

He then explained, "I said exactly the same thing when Tina told me that she believed in Christus alone."

Now Urtzi countered, "Well, maybe you should have listened. Maybe Tina did die prematurely, and her life would have been spared if she had not angered the gods too."

Angus shook his head. "No, I said such things to them. I said to Julius her carer and to her that she had been exiled by the gods as punishment for her exclusive faith. But the shining light on her face, the commitment she exemplified to Julius as a father rather than a servant, his ethical treatment of her when he might have abused her living all alone with no one to stop him - there was something so different about them."

He was quiet and thoughtful. Then he continued. "If I had not hesitated with the doubt I felt about their reasoning, I might have asked to marry my niece. They needed my support. I know it does not sound as if anything worked out ideally. But after I met Aidna who loved Tina so, and who came to find me and ask for my help because of how Tina had reached out to her so kindly, then I began to think about the false claims of Roman and Celtic religion. You experienced that same kindness, Urtzi. You said you called Tina "Pura Lux" (Pure Light). She did shine in the darkness.

After Aidna and I discussed it, we could not deny how we felt anymore about false gods. The manmade gods sound like selfish human beings. But the Christian God is not selfish like a person. There is no darkness in the Christian God. We do not want to serve a selfish god. We want to serve a self-sacrificial God whose holy ways surpass our moral weakness and lack of spiritual understanding."

Urtzi and Esuvia did not argue. They were not ready to commit to a discussion, but they could not deny that Angus and Aidna had a very different spirit about them. Now that it was revealed that the beloved friend Urtzi had received from and observed at a distance was a follower of Christus, there was nothing he could do but marvel. He had grieved over her possible death for years. Now he saw the love she so freely gave from an entirely different perspective. His eyes glittered as he pondered it with a new sense of wonder.

Respectfully, Aidna and Angus did not press the conversation any further. The fire crackled, and a peace ensued after all that had transpired.

10

Reflections in Time

Cast your bread upon the waters, for after many days you will find it again. - Ecclesiastes 11:1 NIV

"Are we judging the gods?" Esuvia pondered as she and Aidna knelt by the river washing the breakfast dishes.

"I understand what you mean, but we felt the opposite is true. We felt it was time to judge ourselves and be honest about why we would want to follow such gods. When we saw that their characteristics were just like flawed humans, we believed there was a higher way to which we should submit." Aidna paused. "Christus called it the water of life. If you want that water, Esuvia, we will pray with you." Aidna reached for Esuvia's hand and firmly gripping it added, "And for some reason, I think I should offer you my pendant."

Esuvia slowly rose and stared with wonder at the pendant Aidna wore, and then at the current of water moving from the sea. She remembered throwing her locket into the sea and felt as if she had received an answer from something bigger than herself. Her heart pounded with hope, but she needed to express her doubts.

"Why do you think such awful things happened to Tina?" Esuvia looked into Aidna's face.

"Awful things happen to everyone, Su. I used to pray for the bereaved. Then, I realized that all of us are bereaved, even from birth. There is always someone missing from our lives - a grandparent, a neighbour who might have been there, a community leader who would have improved things for everyone ... even before we are born, people we need for our best journey on earth die," Aidna stated.

"Everyone dies," Esuvia whispered. She heard a twig snap behind her and whirled round to see Urtzi there. His face reflected what he had just heard.

The rest of the morning was shadowed by the conversation about death. Urtzi's face was troubled, and even Esuvia felt anxious about the journey of childbearing. Since her mother had died in childbirth, it seemed her chances of difficulty might be increased.

The group set out in silence but with resolve to face the truth about Tina's fate when they reached the villa. No one smiled. It was a sombre procession on the road.

It was nearly evening when Urtzi spied his hut through some trees in the distance. He called out to stop the horses. Then, he was running through the sheep-shorn grass to the river.

Esuvia leapt down and ran after him, catching his hand. It felt jarring and somehow empty to be dashing toward a deserted hut. But perhaps some important memories there would be stirred for Urtzi. Angus and Aidna waited with their daughter on the road.

The sun was hitting the water just at the right moment, and it sparkled. At any other time of day, it would bear a different mood and different faces every hour in the changing light. But at that moment, the hope of childhood was reflected to Urtzi in creation. Urtzi and Esuvia stood beside the stream in silence.

"I see why I settled by the sea," Urtzi murmured after a while. "I love the water."

Esuvia squeezed his hand and smiled up at him. He looked down and remembered the moment he first saw her on the shore, looking up at him in the same way. He felt gratitude. "I have much for which I should give thanks," he said. "I have had many blessings and bright moments."

"The river led you to the sea," Esuvia noted the symbolism.

They were within half a mile of the villa. As they rode onwards, Urtzi confessed, "I was blinded by my hatred of the wolves. I meant well, but my bitterness consumed me. I would not have fallen in the trap Maglocunos laid for me if I had not let darkness overwhelm me. I was not thinking of you."

"It was all so strange, I wonder if it really happened. Maglocunos seemed like a character from a children's scary tale. None of it seems real," Esuvia reflected.

"Do you think you met me in a nightmare?" Urtzi laughed.

"I think it truly happened, but yes, it seems as if I joined you in a nightmare."

"A living nightmare?" Urtzi wondered.

"Until yesterday, I would have thought Maglocunos was an evil god, or that the gods sent that tortured monster to punish us. But Angus and Aidna's worldviews are affecting my interpretations," Esuvia answered. "I am not sure exactly how, but different perspectives are beginning to seem possible."

Urtzi agreed, "I know what you mean."

Now, they were ascending a slight incline. Urtzi knew that the villa was over the rise. They paused the horses and then, without hesitation, Urtzi leapt down with Esuvia following closely behind.

The remaining steps to the ridge felt heavy. They could hear their heartbeats in their ears. Their temples throbbed with nervous dread.

Then, something unexpected happened. Little Christina climbed from the cart before anyone could stop her. Her hood fell back as she ran, and her golden locks flew behind her in the breeze. It was an eternal moment. Time stood still as the scene of the universal figure of a child running hopefully up over a hill played out before them.

The memories flooded back to Urtzi. Tina's shining presence crossing the fields to find his little brother who collected the food from her, the sun glinting off of her fair head as she carried shawls and bread to them ... all of it came back radiantly before his mind's eye. The light flashed out and overwhelmed the memory of the dark horror of the wolf attack. He then bravely surged forward to face the scene at the villa below. Courage coursed through him as he embraced the understanding that he was alive because of her. And likewise, Christina was also alive because of her aunt - Christina's parents guided to one another by the love of Tina that served as a beacon for them all.

Esuvia followed closely behind Urtzi with determined steps and stopped beside him on the hill, taking in the view with a breathless expression. They stared with wordless parted lips, looked beyond at the glorious unexpected, then looked at one another. The fear of life and death melted away before the wonder, and Urtzi spoke so quietly from his soul, Esuvia heard in the miraculous moment what at any other time might have been inaudible, "We shall live."

And Esuvia gazed into his face seeing that the light upon his visage was not from the setting sun.

11

Chapter 1 Query

The following ten devotionals, called queries, are about resilience. These have been written as a response to this novel about a person finding a way forward. I have spent many moments of my life struggling to feel resilient. These examples of positive outcomes have only been reached through intense daily meditation and thought.

At a wedding, as a tablecloth representing a hospitable home is lifted and then drifts downwards, the groom has a terrible memory triggered. He shocks his new bride with a depressive part of himself that she has never before seen. So begins the story of a desperate journey of discovery on which a couple must embark to save their relationship.

As the author, I am finding that the characters pouring forth in these tales have a deep need to sojourn and discuss things. Their humanity seems to rise to new heights as they go on meditative walks.

As Jesus walked for hundreds of miles with His disciples, we know that so much was discussed. The Book of Exodus records how a nation rose on a 40-year journey out of Egypt and across a wilderness. Later, the Psalms of David who may have sung and prayed to the Lord as he shepherded in the Judean hills were recorded to be prayed by billions of people for thousands of years.

There is a universal significant need for human beings to pilgrimage and ponder aloud what rises from the depths of our souls as we place ourselves intentionally within the vastness of creation to connect with something bigger than ourselves. Perhaps share about pilgrimages, retreats, or meaningful moments during past travels. If you are not within a group, perhaps journal.

12

Chapter 2 Query

The book *Upright and Three Rivers* that precedes *The Boat Builder and the Mosaic Maker* begins with a deep dive into the spiritual life of a Christian young woman named Tina. However, this second book does not discuss Christian faith at the beginning. Set in Roman Britain in the second century AD, it is realistic about the fact that very few in that part of the world knew about Christus yet. The first book is based on an educated guess that some people would have already heard because of the international influences flowing through Roman Britain from merchants and soldiers from North Africa and other Mediterranean areas where Christianity had spread. But the second book is also true to history in that it presents an almost entirely pagan society at that time in Roman Britain.

When the pagan Angi - a healer - emerged, I thought of people I have known who are intuitive and can warmly shepherd others to a better place through a natural gift of wisdom and encouragement. Without these characteristics of caring people throughout human history, how could any of us have ever been born? Surely there have always been glimpses of the humanity of each person because the thumbprint of God is on us all. Consider the role of ancient midwives, for example. As recorded in the book of Exodus, the Egyptian midwives Shiphrah and Puah expressed their God-given humanity by saving many Hebrew infants from total infanticide.

The Christian belief is that we are fallen, but we are meant to bear the image of Creator God. His image should be seen in our humanity. Jesus, the Son of God, came to restore the image of God within us to its rightful reflection. The image of God is perfectly mirrored in Christ Jesus. Jesus came to restore the human race *completely*.

As a Christian, I must daily strive to be more like Jesus and focus on doing His work that I am meant to do. It is all too easy for me to slip into patterns of anxiety like Urtzi who was overwhelmed at the beginning of the story. But it is better to focus on the goal of acting like Jesus and doing good works for Him. These higher thoughts and actions can help to take my eyes off of my doubts and disappointments and place my focus on a meaningful calling.

If you are sharing in a group, you may wish to name a goal of something you can do today in service to Christ. If you are studying individually, you may wish to journal your goal(s).

Give thanks for individuals who reflect deeply meaningful acts of humanity to you.

13

Chapter 3 Query

What do you think the main point of Chapter 3 is? As the author, I am often surprised when I return to previous chapters. I do not always remember what developed in the story at that moment. Having just re-read it, the main point I see is that we can miss out when we make wrongful assumptions about others. Having a different background than another can give a very different context to meanings and interpretations when we converse. Though our communities seem increasingly global, we will always have more to learn about one another.

During my first years living abroad, I had good intentions, but I miscommunicated sometimes. Unfortunately, I was not always asked to explain what I meant. When I was careful to ask questions about what others meant, and when they asked me what I meant, pleasantries flowed more easily, and relationships deepened. I could not control if others asked questions, but I had to learn to do my part asking others questions. Prayer, the peace of letting the Lord still the waves of anxiety, and trusting in the Holy Spirit as guide helped me with this.

Esuvia was humbled when she saw the humanity of Ness and realized that she could actually learn more from Ness than Ness required of her. When Esuvia grew in her respect for Ness, Esuvia became a happier person.

This reminds me of the Shaker hymn "Simple Gifts". Try finding a recording of this song and its lyrics. Ponder whether its message suits the lesson Esuvia learned from Ness. Enjoy meditative time with the Lord.

14

Chapter 4 Query

The marriage between Urtzi and Esuvia is brand new. They have just experienced what it is like to move away for a time from the stabilizing effect of a community that has supported their union. And then, they have their sleep disrupted by a new baby. Though it is not their own baby, an argument ensues as the effect is felt of waking up in the middle of the night in the home of their young friends tending to their child.

New marriages are often faced with multiple transitions. One or both spouses may move to a new location far from a well-known support system and may also change jobs. If children are in the picture, the marriage relationship may be neglected for the urgent needs of the very young. Couples may be thrown into challenging discoveries about one another that they were not anticipating. These are all strenuous demands. Faced with such tests, one wonders if Urtzi and Esuvia's relationship will survive.

When I began writing this book series, I pondered if there were any way to make symbolic references to the relationship between Christ Jesus and His Church, His Holy Bride. Perhaps some readers may see some connections. I hope you are able to glean inspiring messages about that from these books.

And now, if you will allow me, I shall shift gears a bit. When considering the topic of marriage, it is important for Christians to remember something Jesus said about the signs of the end times. Matthew 24:37-39 states,

"As it was in the days of Noah, so it will be at the coming of the Son of Man. For in the days before the flood, people were eating and drinking, marrying and giving in marriage, up to the day Noah entered the ark; and they knew nothing about what would happen until the flood came and took them all away. That is how it will be at the coming of the Son of Man." (NIV)

This Bible verse sounded confusing to me for many years. Of all of the routine, daily human activities, as well as important, monumental activities that Jesus could have mentioned, why eating and why marriage specifically? But over time spent pondering the meaning, it has occurred to me that what Jesus was describing about end-time feasting and marriage sounds like consumeristic attitudes.

What do you think? Are we treating the most sacred parts of life like a range of products to which we feel entitled? Can you identify contemporary consumeristic attitudes toward marriage? Destructive patterns cannot change without prayer and fasting.

We were all born. I have felt called to pray for my children since they were conceived, and before, as do so many parents. While praying with two friends when we were all three expecting, I had a vision of my mother's face the first time I saw her. The process of up to twelve thousand generations of humans before us that made it possible for us to exist seems important. What if that chain had been broken? What if we had not been born? Even in early childhood, the concept of having never been born hit me very, very hard. Without our births, there would have been nothing ... no existence ... no experience ... no me ... no you.

Throughout life's journey, we can pray for our loved ones, all generations, and even people we will never meet. As well as occasional, every-few-months total fasts with only water lasting 1-3 days, I feel led to fast from various indulgent foods every day as I take the Lord's power to change the world seriously. Somehow I believe that communicating from my soul to God that I know I am not entitled to every comfort I want aids effective prayer. I actually feel better when I sacrifice indulging, and pray instead.

I know that my example is not the best one. Christians around the world and in different Christian denominations fast more than what I have described. I only share this because I believe we need to adopt the spiritual practices such as prayer and fasting that Jesus taught about to address the tough spiritual problems we all face. We can follow Jesus's teaching that includes countering impossible ills and evils with prayer and fasting.

It has recently hit me harder than ever before that God came to us and began His life of hardship by being placed in an animal's feedbox. His poor young mother must have looked around at the floor of the barn and realized that the manger infected with cow spittle was the better option. And there He was, allowing a frightened little couple to love Him as their own, accepting their little broken offering, all that they had. And that was only the beginning. The rest of His journey on earth only grew harder as He endured the worst rejection and humiliation known to humankind to bring true restoration to our humanity. And as he journeyed through his most heavily burdened, earthly life, more people left all that they had and followed him uncompromisingly, as Mary and Joseph had done.

Would you consider any of our present indulgent attitudes toward marriage and family life dehumanizing? Would you say that for our best selves to be realized, our best option is to follow the humble, self-sacrificing, obedient, holy Christ - even when we don't like everything that means that we will have to give up? His life is the perfect model, and we cannot do better than that model.

In our meditation and sharing, let us contemplate the characteristics of Jesus's sacrificial life on earth and ask ourselves how we can apply it better to ourselves.

15

Chapter 5 Query

Chapter 5 ends with Urtzi marching into a dangerous trap laid by a psychopathic killer. Urtzi erroneously interprets a sign that Maglocunos is the leader who will help him kill wolves, as Urtzi has always dreamed of slaughtering packs of wolves. Maglocunos has a devil and easily spies Urtzi's weakness.

How many times do we misinterpret signs because of our own desires that we may not recognize as misguided? I share the following account for both individuals and parents in the hopes that it is helpful to someone out there.

In high school, I was passionately following a calling to study music. However, I wonder if I misinterpreted signs about which activities were the best for developing my gifts. I left two of my most life-giving opportunities - one of which was cross country with a team of extremely good girls who would have made the best possible friends I could have had. Another loss was the energy the hard sport increased for me. Never did I make better grades in high school than the semester I had to balance cross country running with everything else. Because of the healthy, challenging exercise, my brain and body were much more awake than any other time in my life up to that point. Cross country definitely would not have detracted from my music development. I miscalculated that it would.

I also left a community Christian youth choir that was a far better opportunity than any other choir I knew. The long evenings we spent sharing devotionals across our denominational cultures were the most edifying discussions I heard in those long four years of high school. But again, I wrongly assumed that the late evenings were too costly. To be fair, my family lived quite far from the venue in which we rehearsed, and I did take the needs of family members transporting me late at night into consideration. I did not quit for selfish reasons, but I do think that I was misguided in my decision-making.

Unpleasant things happened to me after I quit those two activities, among which was feeling bullied in a competitive educational choir I joined. Again, to be fair to myself, I joined that educational choir because I believed it was a necessary part of university preparation - university being something my parents lovingly required. On the other hand, that competitive choir seemed not only educational, but also glamorous to all of us, and looks can be deceiving.

However, because the one cross country season and the brief community youth choir experience were so outstanding, the seeds literally bore good fruit for the rest of my life. My life is better today because of cross country and community youth choir in 9th grade (British year 10). I just wish I had more good memories like those, and fewer sad ones. Though I sincerely tried to follow Christ Jesus every day in my personal life, I may have misread the signs because of insecurities I did not understand within myself. Teenage years are so difficult, and all young people learn many things the hard way on their journey.

Maybe you can think of a time in your life when you misread a sign you believed to be from God because you were looking for the answers in the wrong places for misguided reasons. Take time to share if you wish within your group, or perhaps journal if you are studying privately. Remember to forgive yourself. When we learn from bad experiences, we may still gain through growth in empathy toward the struggles of all.

16

Chapter 6 Query

In studying Chapter 6, what comes to my thoughts are examples of moments recorded in the Bible of God changing His mind. There are accounts of people appealing to God, and God changing an outcome as a result. One example is that of Hezekiah in II Kings 20.

In this passage, King Hezekiah was dying, and the prophet Isaiah son of Amoz prophesied that Hezekiah would die. Hezekiah then appealed to God for healing. Hezekiah's faithfulness in his leadership as king of Israel had been outstanding. He had brought his nation much closer to God. God then recognized Hezekiah's prayer for healing and gave him fifteen more years of life on earth.

Urtzi is certain he is about to be killed, but Esuvia and the slaves intervene, and his life is saved. Contemplate a time you or someone you know had a deep spiritual certainty of an outcome, but after intercessory prayer, circumstances changed or improved. If you cannot think of an example, ponder a time that an unexpected turn of events changed lives for the better.

I was sad when we moved away from the lovely primary school where my daughter began her education. We answered a calling to work where she was born and began school, and we chose the school because of a shared vision of the kingdom of God. When we felt the Lord say it was better spiritually for us to live elsewhere for a time, I never stopped missing the innocence and beauty of that school. But when my daughter was twenty and studied abroad, she got to return to that very tree-lined street to live a few metres from where she first began school. In truth, had we not left following God, that sweet moment of return could never have happened.

That is only one small, personal example of a restoration of circumstances in some way. Many other examples of restoration and many kinds of healing are possible. Perhaps you have a story to share of restoration and/or healing that may bring hope to someone else.

Only God can see the arc of all that has been and is to come. Pray that God will help us trust Him more with our past, present, and future.

17

Chapter 7 Query

Life can come full circle. Sometimes we are so surprised by a resolution to a seemingly unsolveable problem, we may find ourselves asking, "What just happened?" When we are young adults, we think that life will last forever, and disappointments can seem like a permanent scar we will never be able to forget. But then, another generation is born, and there is not only new hope for the future, but past lessons from hardship we endured can be applied to a better tomorrow for them.

Urtzi never dreamed that on a road he would one day meet a child - Aurora Christina - who would never have been born had it not been for the influence of Tina on her parents, Aidna and Angus. By the same token, Angus never dreamed that a young adult was contributing as a husband and a good worker who may never have lived to adulthood if Tina had not provided him with food and hope after he was orphaned.

Though these examples may seem extreme, I have found that as the generation after us grows up, examples such as these are not extreme after all. When we are intentional about following Christ Jesus and sow into what He offers us to do, we may sow in tears, but later, we truly will reap somehow in joy. This is a Biblical promise. (See Psalm 126:5-6.) If this inspires thoughts, perhaps share within your group, or if studying privately, prayerfully journal. Blessings to you.

18

Chapter 8 Query

"To cry and live till I die for all the joy and pain that life can hold ... "

As a music teacher, it is ridiculous for me to think that any recital will ever go completely without casualty. One recital in a gloriously peaceful May garden atmosphere was preceded with a puppy throwing off our preparation schedule by chewing through a 100-foot extension cord, just two hours before the guests arrived. But who am I to think that an artistic expression of our humanity will somehow go off without any mistakes? True life includes mistakes, and artistic presentations reflect this, somehow. I have seen unusually gifted, national award-winning ballerinas slip and fall down in a performance, then shake off the chalk dust with a laugh and dance through another decade. The most inspiring stories of athletes are about resilience after failure, because we all fail. Why else would we watch the Olympics?

In the spring of my 4th grade year, (British year 5), I played a short classical piece in a music recital and was so nervous, I kept speeding up faster and faster, absolutely flying through it, racing out of control like a wheel rolling down a steep incline! At the end, I let out a visible sigh of relief, and the audience burst into laughter. I imagined I could feel the embarrassment of my parents in the car as we rode home.

But I loved that piece, so I kept playing it, and entered it in a school talent show six months later. I did not win, but I gave a good presentation and received a blue ribbon. That would have made a nice story about courage and the reward of improvement, but that is not the end of this true story!

I just loved that classical piece, so a year later in the 6th grade, I entered the school talent show again and played both that piece and another piece I had been learning. This time, I won **first place** in the talent show and was allowed to advance to a regional talent show in which I gave another good performance.

Now, what if I had given up after a disappointing music recital in the 4th grade? What if I had quit taking music lessons and carried around a sad story of why piano recitals are bad for children for the rest of my life? That would have been true failure. I would never have gone to music school, finished two degrees, taught family music groups for ten years to hundreds of people in Oxford, England, and enjoyed running a private music teaching studio for as long as I wanted to throughout my life. I am thankful my parents would never have allowed me to quit because I had a disappointing experience. Anything we achieve in life begins with a journey full of mountains of disappointment, accidents, heartache, humiliation, and injuries. The key is to keep our eyes on the goal and keep moving toward the goal. *And because music teaching was a calling*, I could throw my burdens on the Lord's shoulders when the journey seemed almost unbearable, which it did at certain times.

It is a good thing to get to a place where we can view mistakes positively as an opportunity for growth. Teachers and parents must learn to shepherd others through those experiences. As Urtzi faces his future as a father, he sees an expanse filled with many variations of highs and lows, and he resolves to finish the race to completion for the others he loves.

Meditate and share in writing or with others a mistake through which growth came, turning a dead end into a possibility.

19

Chapter 9 Query

Angus and Aidna decided that they did not want to serve selfish gods. The gods they had always known about sounded as if they had wrongful human personality characteristics such as pride.

The Christian God sounded unselfish and had a different effect on His followers. The people they met who followed Christus seemed to become more self-sacrificing, other-focused human beings. That was the observation of Angus and Aidna.

All people, including Christians, sin and sometimes behave selfishly. Some non-Christians you know may be extremely caring, unselfish people. But the goal of growing as a Christian is to become more like Jesus and make the world better as a result of obeying the teachings of Jesus and His leading.

If one is serving selfish ambition, one will reap the rewards of that which may begin with glamour and gold, but along the way, will result in the loss of the things that money cannot buy - the things that truly matter.

If someone is seeking God, they will find Him. (See Matthew 7:7.) He came as an unselfish servant of all people in the form of Jesus. Jesus is the pure reflection of Father God. That means the character of God is an unselfish, other-focused Being. How are we seeking God?

20

Chapter 10 Query

What do you think that Urtzi and Esuvia saw from the top of the hill? Do you think that this chapter called "Reflections in Time" is about an event happening at that moment? Perhaps so, but perhaps it is open-ended.

This story is fictional, but the Holy Bible is filled with truth. Biblical truth is always so profound, we cannot fathom the multi-layers, and will continue discovering more depths as we ponder God's words throughout life's journey. So, I do not have an answer for you about whether Urtzi and Esuvia's vision is happening in real time, just as I cannot answer how Biblical prophecy may unfold eschatologically.

Discuss with others how Biblical truth you have studied may have unfolded for you in layers and layers throughout your life, or write about it in your journal.

21

Chapter 1 Study

Vocabulary

Please define each word and use with a sentence.

Identify words with a Latin root.

1. Ethereal
2. Countenance
3. Passage (of a house)
4. To retch
5. Envision
6. Inanimate
7. Barricade
8. Surf (noun)
9. Disdain
10. Fein
11. To jest
12. Berth
13. Plight
14. Stature
15. Periwinkle (colour)
16. Tresses
17. Poignant

18. Depict
19. Banter
20. Helm
21. To field
22. Vise

Latin Names

1.. Esuvia
2. Adrian
3. Tessera
4. Priscilla
5. Vasco
6. Vallum Aelium

Basque Name

1. Urtzi

Social Studies Research

1.Research and write two paragraphs describing a Roman wedding.
2.Research and describe a modest ancient Roman house.
3.What is "Basque"?

Arts

1. Read an article about small boat building. Discuss in a short essay of 3-5 paragraphs.
2. Read an article about Roman mosaics. Discuss in a short essay of 3-5 paragraphs.

Snack

As part of the ancient ceremony, Roman brides smeared animal fat on the doorpost of their new home. A popular food that is made with animal fat is gravy. Try making some sausage gravy and biscuits. Alternatively, find a recipe for Wedding Cookies and bake!

22

Chapter 2 Study

Vocabulary

Please define each word and use within a sentence.
Identify words with a Latin root.

1. Herbalist
2. Counterintuitive
3. Pilgrimage
4. Listless
5. Template
6. Scour
7. Compensate
8. Plantain
9. Tangible
10. Traverse
11. Traipsed
12. Expanse

Latin

1. Angitia
2. Circe

Social Studies

Angi is a healer. Her methods seem like that of someone intuitive and knowledgeable of human psychology. What did the Romans know about psychology? Write two paragraphs.

Snack

Herbal teas. Angi used lavender, camomile, sage, and bay leaf. Choose one of these herbal teas and enjoy the warm beverage. (Bay leaf tea is simply made by steeping dry bay leaves in hot water.)

Angi and Esuvia shopped for cabbage, barley, plantain, and meat. Prepare corned beef and cabbage and barley bread for lunch! Plantain can be found at a local supermarket and fried in a delicious batter in 15 minutes. Research recipes.

Broad plantain leaves probably grow in the grass in your back garden. Research how this plant has been used for food and medicine.

23

Chapter 3 Study

Vocabulary

Please define each word and use within a sentence.
Identify words with a Latin root.

1. succumb
2. comradery
3. adamantly
4. ensuing
5. encased
6. downy
7. etiquette
8. elaborate
9. commonality
10. wince
11. deluge
12. rudimentary
13. empathetic
14. pretense
15. abode

Celtic

1. Erecura
2. Aife
3. Cu
4. Ness

Latin

1. Juno
2. Junius
3. Dubris
4. Durovernum
5. River Tamesis
6. Londinium
7. Brittonic

Geography

1. Download a map of Roman Britain or go to your local library and study a reference book of maps of Roman Britain. Locate Portus Dubris, the River Tamesis, the North Sea, and Londinium.
2. Do we know the direction of the current between the North Sea and the River Tamesis to Londinium during the age of Roman Britain? No, we do not. Find evidence to support this statement.
3. Research farm animals that thrive on lime-rich grass. Why is this so?
4. Describe what "The Downs" refers to in southern England.
5. Research some items that might have been imported by ships to Roman Britain. List five to ten items.
6. Research the depth of the River Thames. Describe setting poles or quants and discuss their use with boats.

Language Arts

1. Research ancient storytelling. Write two paragraphs describing why it was important.
2. Imagine you are sitting around an evening campfire with friends and make up a short story. Write it down in a stream of consciousness. Do not overthink it.

Snack

Cu and Ness were shepherds. Traditional Greek gyros are made with lamb, as are many other Greek and Lebanese dishes.
If you do not want to experiment with cooking, try one from a restaurant of your choice. If you are like us, you already know where to find this delicious food!

24

Chapter 4 Study

Vocabulary

Please define and use within a sentence.

Identify words with a Latin root.

1. Revel
2. Contort
3. Surmise
4. Exude
5. Dredge

British English	**American English**
1. Apologise	1. Apologize

Social Studies

1. Study a time zone map. What time in the very early morning do you think Cu, Ness, Aife, Urtzi, and Esuvia rose to find bright daylight in the month of Junius in southern Britannia?

Science

1. Research botulism as a risk of carcasses in drinking water. Write one paragraph.

Snack - Trailmix is a fun snack to share with others on a hike. Esuvia tries to coax Urtzi to open up more by offering him some raisins as they walk. Experiment with making your own trail mix recipe. Include dried fruit, cereals, chocolate chips, marshmallows, or whatever you enjoy. Share with friends.

25

Chapter 5 Study

Vocabulary

Please define and use within a sentence.

Identify words with a Latin root.

1. Metaphorical
2. Inconspicuous
3. Disheveled
4. Unkempt
5. Implausible
6. Perimeter
7. Formidable
8. Cacophony
9. Leer
10. Deter
11. Maleficence
12. Feign
13. Implore
14. Rant
15. Desist
16. Strewn

Latin

1. Lupus
2. Canis

Celtic/English

Maglocunos

British English	**American English**
1. Realise	1.Realize

Geography

1. Urtzi and Esuvia have a view of part of the Thames River Valley. Research the Thames River Valley and write two paragraphs.
2. Do you live near a river valley? Name and describe the river valley closest to where you live.

History

1. The "Maglocunos" in this story is fictional. There are records of a historical figure named "Maglocunos". Research who he was and write a paragraph describing what you discovered.

Science

1. The name "Maglocunos" means "king of hounds". In the story *The Mosaic Maker and the Boat Builder,* Maglocunos trained his dogs to be fierce. Do you have a dog? Research how to shape a dog's behaviour whether you own a dog or not. Dogs are everywhere, and it is important to understand them as much as possible. Write two paragraphs.

Snack

Urtzi and Esuvia stumbled onto the property of Maglocunos while out searching for farms that sold fresh produce. Do you live near a local farm where fresh produce is for sale? Try to acquire local produce such as fruit from an orchard. Does it seem hearty? Is the taste more fresh or rich, or not really? Give thanks for your food.

26

Chapter 6 Study

Vocabulary

Please define and use within a sentence.

Identify words with a Latin root.

1. Exude
2. Comradery
3. To nurture
4. Emanate
5. Stealthy
6. To rend
7. To wield
8. Premonition
9. Recount
10. Fray

Social Studies

1. Review slavery in ancient Rome. Write a two paragraph summary.
2. Urtzi's grandparents migrated from the Vasco (Basque) region before Urtzi was born in Roman Britain. After all of his family members passed away, Urtzi travelled on the Tamesis (River Thames) on a raft he made. He then

worked on a vessel sailing to Portus Dubris (Dover) There he would settle and learn to build the boats he had become so fascinated watching as he lived in a hut by the Tamesis with his brother throughout his childhood.

Urtzi's grandparents were immigrants. Research immigration in the ancient Roman Empire and the attitudes of the Roman government toward migration. Write a 500-700 word essay.

3. There is a fictional comment at the end of chapter 6 that wild dogs remained on the isle for 1,000 years! Research "The Isle of Dogs" located in London, England. Describe two theories of why this peninsula is named "The Isle of Dogs".

Snack

Research "pinxtos" (Basque Style Tapas) and prepare your own. Items you may need could include baguettes, cheese, smoked salmon, boiled eggs, olives, tomatoes, red peppers and a small skewer or long toothpicks to hold them together. Delicious.

27

Chapter 7 Study

Vocabulary

Please define and use within a sentence.

Identify words with a Latin root.

1. Transpire
2. Surmise
3. Reverie
4. Inevitable
5. An aside (in conversation)
6. Deviously
7. Entourage
8. Languish
9. Berate
10. Authoritative
11. Quell
12. Impasse
13. Writhe
14. Condolence

Latin

1. Pura
2. Pura Lux

Research for Extra Credit

Urtzi named Tina "Pura Lux", meaning "Pure Light". Why could Urtzi have not called Tina "Angel" or "Angel of Light"? Research the etymology of the word "Angel'. Refer to four influential languages including Old English.

Snack

Tina's gift to Urtzi and his brother was bread wrapped in shawls. Today is a good day to bake fresh bread of your choice. Enjoy some for you, and share some with a neighbour. Think about the presentation of the bread. Perhaps give it in a basket, platter, or piece of cloth that bears meaning.

28

Chapter 8 Study

Vocabulary

Please identify and use within a sentence.

Identify words with a Latin root.

1. Pallid
2. Agitate
3. Jibes
4. Sojourner

Grammar

Describe when "anymore" should be one word, and when two.

Literary Style

"... to cry and live till he died for all the joy and pain that life can hold" is a loaded statement. Write a paragraph describing what this means and why it is used at this point of the story.

Pastoral Care

Chapter 8 includes a description of the grief the group experiences when they believe that Triana may have died. Have you ever discussed grief sensitivity with a youth worker or other leader? Grief sensitivity is a good topic for a youth group or class to explore. Perhaps you have been through bereavement of a friend or family member and can share with others what helped you at that time.

If not, set aside a time when you can talk to a leader about how to support a friend dealing with grief.

Snack

Replace snack time with a discussion and act of service. First, consider what "Lent" is. The season of Lent in many churches is an observation of the grief that Jesus experienced for the losses of creation, and our own responsibility to also grieve over sin and the loss it causes in this world.
To observe Lent, Christians may sacrifice something such as portions of food. A favourite food to give up during Lent is chocolate, but there are innumerable ways to observe sacrifice beyond giving up chocolate. Some people give up gossip. Some give up "screen time".

Letting go of something to which we feel entitled is a good first step toward the humility that leads to spiritual growth. A key spiritual exercise during Lent is to say a prayer for someone or the world whenever you miss the thing you have temporarily given up.

After you have discussed the topic of feelings of entitlement and the need for self-sacrifice as a Christian exercise, plan to offer food to someone else. If you can contribute to meals for someone during illness or bereavement, this is an opportunity to grow in the humility that is the cloak of a Christian. We must submit to being clothed in the humility of Christ Jesus at all times, whether we observe Lent or not, and that humility bears the fruit of humble acts of service to others who are suffering.

29

Chapter 9 Study

Vocabulary

Please define and use within a sentence.
Identify words with a Latin root.

1. Dumbfounded
2. Paraphernalia
3. Exemplify
4. Ethical
5. Exiled
6. Surpass

Religion

What is exclusive Christian faith?

Research

1. Research the locket Roman girls wore until marriage.
2. Research the sign of the Ichthus and how it was used as a secret symbol in the early church.

Snack

A good deal of discussion takes place around campfires as the two young families join and begin to travel together. Prepare a lunch around a fire pit if you have one available or have a picnic today. Eat whatever you like best in either of these settings, and contemplate how easy conversation can be when shared outside in a natural environment.

30

Chapter 10 Study

Vocabulary

Please define and use within a sentence.
Identify words with a Latin root.
1. Somber (American spelling) or Sombre (British spelling)
2. Visage

Language Research

Many American English words are spelled differently than British English words. Research why this is and summarize.

Art

The scene of a child or person standing on top of a hill looking into the distance inspires thoughts that can be universally shared. Many people would say that such a scene inspires hope. Others may say it is about awe and wonder, or longing for something beyond ourselves.
Study some prints or photos of art and discuss the wordless messages conveyed. For example, a painting of a vase of flowers touches memories within many people's minds of a moment of the day when fresh or silk flowers were placed on a table,

and how it made them feel. This would ring true on almost every continent of the planet, except in extreme weather conditions. Fruit bowls, water scenes, and many other subjects can evoke feelings that human beings share in common. Though it can also work in an alternative direction by sometimes evoking feelings that highlight differences in cultural experiences, this exercise is about how art draws us together when it highlights a shared human experience. Study and then list some subjects that probably fascinate and evoke similar emotions in many people.

Snack

Something about what Urtzi and Esuvia see from the top of the hill is celebratory because they are suddenly overwhelmed by spiritual light. Today is a good day to celebrate the gift of hope. What food do you think represents celebration? Personally, I would like a slice of delicious cake! Enjoy the completion of this book and the work you have shared with a celebratory food of your choice. If you are in a group, perhaps plan a party, and ask each person to bring their favourite celebratory food.

www.ingramcontent.com/pod-product-compliance
Ingram Content Group UK Ltd.
Pitfield, Milton Keynes, MK11 3LW, UK
UKHW061023310726
14090UKWH00023B/41

* 9 7 9 8 8 6 9 2 0 2 1 1 6 *